Growing up near the beach,
Annie West spent lots of time
observing tall, burnished lifeguards—
early research! Now she spends
her days fantasising about gorgeous
men and their love-lives. Annie
has been a reader all her life. She
also loves travel, long walks, good
company and great food. You can
contact her at annie@annie-west.com
or via PO Box 1041, Warners Bay,
NSW 2282, Australia.

ONE NIGHT WITH HER FORGOTTEN HUSBAND

ANNIE WEST

MILLS & BOON

First published in Great Britain 2022
by Mills & Boon, an imprint of HarperCollins*Publishers* Ltd,
1 London Bridge Street, London, SE1 9GF

www.harpercollins.co.uk

HarperCollins*Publishers*
1st Floor, Watermarque Building,
Ringsend Road, Dublin 4, Ireland

Large Print edition 2022

One Night with Her Forgotten Husband © 2022 Annie West

ISBN: 978-0-263-29551-1

08/22

This story is dedicated to the
Newcastle Romance Writers Group.

Here's to marvellous plots,
words that flow like warm honey
and, above all, camaraderie.

CHAPTER ONE

A SHOUT DREW Angelo's attention. He stepped through the open French doors and saw Enzo, the gardener, leaning over the balustrade of the lowest garden terrace.

Enzo was staring down towards the sea. Then he spun around, saw Angelo and waved urgently.

'A body!'

Angelo frowned. Enzo's eyesight was cloudy and he was due to have cataract surgery soon. He must be mistaken. Yet he repeated it. 'There's a body on the beach.'

Angelo sprinted towards him. With every step he told himself it was simply a stray tourist, drawn to sun themself on the island's unique pale pink sand. Though, given the strengthening wind and ominous clouds spreading across the brilliant blue sky, they'd picked an odd time. The forecast was for a savage storm.

It must be a stranger who didn't know the cove was private and had swum ashore from a boat. Though every local boat owner respected Angelo Ricci's privacy. None would allow an outsider near his home.

Angelo slammed to a stop beside his gardener, staring down at the body. A woman, lying face down at one end of the beach.

His breath backed up in his throat, his brain cataloguing every detail.

Any thought that she might be sunbathing died. She lay mainly in the water, slender bare legs extended. The lap of waves made her oversized white T-shirt lift and ripple around her hips but it was the only sign of movement. She lay utterly, heart-stoppingly still. Nor was she lying totally on sand. Her head and one outflung arm rested on an outcrop of rocks above the water. It was clear, even from here, that her clutching hand was limp.

'Call the doctor!'

Angelo vaulted the balustrade to land in a crouch at the bottom of the first set of steps on the path down to the beach. He felt his bent knees absorb the shock. A second later he rose and pivoted, hurtling down the next set of steps that made the almost sheer rock face negotiable.

Mere minutes must have passed since he'd heard Enzo yell. Yet it felt like a lifetime.

Perhaps, for the woman below it *was* a lifetime. Each second could mean the difference between life and death.

Angelo felt each beat of his pulse as if in slow

motion while his brain raced. He recognised the clarity of senses, the hyper-awareness of his adrenaline surge, from previous crises.

The last time had been while climbing in the Dolomites in the north of the country. When he and his climbing partner rescued a couple of beginners who'd got into trouble. One had broken a few bones in a fall and the other had frozen with fear. It had taken a lot of ingenuity to get the pair to safety.

Angelo's feet touched sand. He shunted the memory to the back of his mind as he powered towards the rocks.

She mightn't be dead. Surely there was a possibility...

Angelo dropped to his knees, careful not to touch her as he scanned both the woman and the empty beach. No footprints. No evidence anyone had been here, except her.

Even above the waterline the sodden T-shirt clung to her body and her hair was wet. So she hadn't been here long. It looked as if she'd walked or dragged herself partly clear of the sea before collapsing.

He reached out and gently circled her wrist with his fingers, searching for a pulse.

It was there, weak at first, but when he shifted his grip, stronger and even.

Relief rose like a warm tide. Angelo sat back on his heels and heaved in a slow breath. Alive and not obviously injured. From what he could see.

He surveyed her surroundings, the damp sand and dark rock. No sign of blood. He scanned her bare arms and legs, noting she had the smooth, unblemished skin of youth. There were a few freckles on her arms and, though lightly tanned, her pale colouring hinted she was likely a tourist rather than a local. Olive skin was more common here in the south of Italy.

Dare he move her? Turn her over?

He had no idea if she'd injured her back or head on the rocks that ran out into the sea from this end of the beach. Better to wait for a medical professional.

Angelo lifted his gaze to the cobalt sea, growing choppy as he watched. The mainland was close yet far enough to prevent people swimming across. There wasn't a boat in sight. But now he thought about it, he'd heard a speedboat earlier, in far too close to the rocks. But if she'd been on a boat, where was it now?

This was no time for speculation. He leaned over the woman and carefully lifted some strands of wet brown hair from her face.

She didn't move.

He reached again, drawing more tresses back

behind her ear. The action uncovered the sweep of long eyelashes against the curve of her cheek.

Abruptly Angelo sat back, heart thrumming against his ribs. His breath was a snatch of air that made his lungs ache because he forgot to exhale.

He frowned. This was no time for flights of fantasy. He had an injured woman to deal with. He had to discover how badly injured.

Carefully he slipped his hand under the mass of wet hair and lifted it all off this side of her face.

He almost dropped it as he saw what lay beneath.

Shock jolted him. As if lightning had struck through him.

There was no blood. Yet what he saw horrified him.

His gaze traced the slant of her cheekbone, the line of her nose and delicately carved nostril, down to full lips that were too pale.

His hand shook.

Because he knew her.

It was impossible that she was here.

Yet there was no doubt. He'd know that profile anywhere.

He remembered leaning over her as the early morning sun flooded his bedroom. She'd stretched back into his aroused body, a feline smile of satisfaction curving those lips as she rubbed herself against him.

Angelo blinked, dispelling the memory.

Then he frowned. A smattering of freckles stood out against the unnatural pallor of her face. Those were new.

And her eyebrow looked different, still beautifully arched but more natural-looking than when he'd seen her last.

Slowly he released her hair so it fell behind her ear, leaving her face clear. He snatched his hand away. It tingled as if stung by unseen ants.

Of course she looks different. It's been five years.

Yet she didn't look older. If anything she looked younger than before.

Angelo snorted, feeling warmth begin to trickle back into his shock-numbed body. She'd spent a fortune, both in time and products, to maintain her looks. She'd claimed it was necessary because of her work, but he knew she'd been just as motivated by vanity. She'd see ageing as a personal affront.

Which didn't explain what she was doing here, of all places.

His eyes narrowed as he caught a smudge of colour on his hand. Blood?

Reluctantly he bent forward and there, if he

wasn't mistaken, was a patch of darker colour in her wet hair.

He was just reaching out to investigate when her eyelashes fluttered. Or did he imagine it? Angelo stared, alert to any movement. There it was again, the tiniest stirring.

A wrinkle appeared on her smooth brow and tiny vertical lines appeared above her nose. To his horror Angelo found himself thinking the frown looked almost cute on that clear, guileless face.

Guileless? His mouth twisted in a grimace of bitter derision.

That was one thing he couldn't accuse her of. This woman was an opportunist. Self-obsessed. Conniving.

She was an outright liar.

In fact, now he was here, on his knees beside her, he began to wonder about the convenient *accident* that had washed her up on his private beach. It was a little too unbelievable, surely?

Angelo Ricci was many things but gullible wasn't one of them. Once, definitely, and to his cost. But no longer. He'd learned distrust thoroughly and brutally.

If it were any other woman, he'd take her at face value. But not her. Was the blood in her hair actually some sort of dye?

Her frown deepened and tiny grooves appeared at the corner of her mouth. Her expression spoke of pain. Or the pretence of it.

Maybe she wasn't injured at all. Maybe she just feigned it and sensed his scepticism.

But why go to all this bother? She couldn't think he was willing to forget what had passed between them.

Her lashes moved again and she groaned. A soft, heartfelt sound that, despite his suspicion, wrenched at his conscience. Maybe she really was injured.

He watched her swallow, the movement jerky, then her tongue circled her lips.

Angelo moved to sit on the rocks on her other side so he was in full view when she opened her eyes.

Suddenly she did.

He still had a view of only half her face, the other half pressed to the rock, but there was no mistaking what he saw. Only one woman he knew had eyes like that. Eyes the colour of lavender or, she'd told him, the flowers of the jacaranda tree. A stunning colour between blue and purple.

His breath whistled out as his lungs cramped.

She didn't seem to see him straight away. It was only when he moved that her gaze tracked towards his face. Even then he wasn't sure she focused on him. There was no recognition in her features. No start of surprise or satisfaction.

'Hello, Alexa.' His voice was a gravel rumble, dragged out of him despite his will.

She blinked and then, after a moment's blank stare, closed her eyes.

Fear shot through him. Angelo didn't want her here. Wanted never to see her again. But the thought of her dying at his home, on his watch, was another matter.

'Alexa!'

Her frown turned into a scowl and she flinched.

Because she'd hoped for a warmer welcome? Or because she was really in pain? She might have a head injury. On the other hand she could be shamming. Either was possible.

'Alexa. Speak to me.'

Despite his doubts, concern filled him. Damn it, he didn't know whether to leave her as she was for fear of doing some damage or carry her up to the house.

Her lips moved. 'Not Alexa.' He had to lean in close, almost touching her, to hear the slow whisper. 'Ally.'

Angelo stared. She'd changed her name? But Ally would be a short form of Alexa.

Yet the woman he'd known hated being called

anything but her full name. It was her brand as well as her personal name and she insisted on promoting it assiduously.

He heard a shout and looked up to the people picking their way down the cliff path. Medical help was on its way.

Relief stirred. The doctor would do what was necessary. Angelo would find out soon enough if her injury was real.

Her mouth was full of cotton wool. Cotton wool that tasted rancid. But the dry, sickening sensation that made her want to gag was nothing compared with the pain. It was so all-encompassing she couldn't pinpoint its source, though she had the mother of all headaches.

She lay there for a lifetime, knowing she was awake, not dreaming, but unable to summon the effort to open her eyes. Because she just knew that would make the hurt even worse.

The pain grew more defined. Her shoulders and arms ached. Her body and legs felt battered. Her hip was on fire. But it was her head… Even thinking about the pain hammering at her skull made it worse.

Dimly she became aware of noise. A rough, rushing sound. Or was that her pulse? Then, from nearby, the sound of someone moving.

Knowing she'd regret it, she opened her eyes. Instantly light jabbed at her in a blinding flash and she squeezed her eyes shut.

Someone spoke. A man with a warm, gentle voice, but she couldn't make out the words.

He spoke again and a firm hand took hers, testing her pulse.

She was hurt. Maybe she was in hospital. The voice spoke again and she frowned. She'd thought at first that she hadn't heard him properly because of the heavy pound of her pulse and her dull stuffed-with-cotton head. Now she realised there was something else. Something she couldn't quite grasp.

'Bene, bene. Sei sveglia.'

She frowned, then regretted it as even that movement sharpened the ache.

'I...' She swiped her mouth with a tongue that felt swollen and clumsy. 'Am I in hospital?' she whispered. Every syllable took effort.

'Not hospital,' a heavily accented voice replied. 'You're in Signor Ricci's home. He brought you up from the beach.'

Slowly she digested that. One word at a time.

She'd been on a beach. She was hurt. Someone had brought her to a house. Her breath exhaled in a fractured rush. 'Thank you.'

'Can you open your eyes?'

Her mouth twisted. Was she ready for more pain? But lying indefinitely in the dark was no real option.

She slitted her eyes open, hissing in a breath at the assault of light. But after a few seconds it got better, almost bearable.

She caught movement and her gaze focused on a thin man with a worn face and kind brown eyes.

'*Bene. Bene.*'

That was what he'd said before. It sounded familiar but as soon as she grasped at it the sense of familiarity faded.

'What...' She swallowed hard. 'What are you saying?'

For a second she caught concern on his face. But then it seemed she'd imagined it. He smiled and something inside her eased. 'Just that you're doing very well.'

A laugh escaped her dry throat. A chuckle more than a laugh and even that was cut short by a shaft of pain. 'I'd hate...' Her words trailed off, then his hand took hers again and she roused. 'Hate to see *poorly* if this is *very well.*'

'You're safe,' he reassured her and he sounded so certain she believed him. Or maybe she didn't have the energy not to. 'You'll be looked after. But first I need to examine you properly.'

The next time she woke the light wasn't so bright and the doctor wasn't there. She was alone in the dimly lit room and didn't know whether to be glad or worried. Her head ached but not so sharply. Nevertheless, she wasn't eager to move. She closed her eyes again, cataloguing how she felt.

Something hovered at the edge of her consciousness. Something disturbing. But that fuzzy feeling was a convenient reason to ignore it for now.

When she felt stronger she'd face whatever it was.

That rushing sound was still there, louder this time. After a while she recognised it as the wind tearing fast around the building. Occasionally it built to a buffeting surge and unease tugged at her. If the weather was this bad she needed to go outside and check on...

But the thought slid away half-formed.

A frown bunched her forehead. What was it she had to do? Why was it so urgent? Something that was her responsibility. Something important.

Whatever it was, it would have to wait. She couldn't pin down the details. Besides, she wasn't sure she had the energy to get up.

Experimentally she lifted one hand and discovered it had become a leaden weight.

At least it moves. At least it's not broken.

Instinctively she lifted her other hand, then twitched her feet, just enough to be sure they'd respond to her mental command. Relief rose.

The doctor had said there was no sign of spinal injury, she recollected now.

Instantly she felt better, remembering that worn face and his genial expression. He'd been gentle but professionally brisk, reassuring her that she'd feel better with sleep. A sigh escaped and she turned her head on the soft pillow.

This was incredibly comfortable for a hospital bed. Still with her eyes closed, she swiped her hand across the mattress. Then one foot. This was no single bed.

What was it he'd said? Something about a beach. Being carried up to a house. She must still be there. Maybe she'd better try getting up after all. She didn't want to be a burden. She'd need to make arrangements to get home.

Again that nagging feeling of something not right tugged at her. Something to do with going home? Anxiety niggled.

'You're awake, then.'

A different voice this time. A man's voice, deep and rich as homemade *dulce de leche*. She could almost taste the luscious caramel, sinfully addic-

tive, on her tongue, just from those few words.
She swallowed and found her mouth dry.

Slowly, wary of that horrible lancing pain, she
slitted open her eyes.

A man stood beside the bed. A tall man with
glossy dark hair. Her gaze tracked from strong
thighs and trim hips in worn denim jeans, up a
long torso that broadened as it went. His pale
polo shirt wasn't tight but she had no trouble
making out the impressive musculature of his
toned, powerful body.

For a second she wondered if this were a dream
after all. This man was...spectacular.

It wasn't just his height and sexy body. Nor his
strong-boned face that had passed *good-looking*
and travelled on into *gorgeous but severe*. There
was a magnetism about him that combined attraction and an air of aloofness.

Her heart gave a mighty thump.

He looked familiar.

Maybe she'd seen him on a billboard—that
beautiful, stern dark face staring up at a moun-
tain peak while he, in rugged climbing gear,
sported the ultimate luxury watch on his wrist.
She could imagine him selling something masculine and extravagantly expensive.

One black eyebrow rose, interrupting her dal-
lying imagination.

'Yes,' she croaked and circled her dry mouth with her tongue. 'Awake again. Though I sort of hoped this…' she waggled her hand to encompass the bed '…was a dream.'

He stood, arms folded, watching her. He didn't even seem to blink. Finally he spoke. 'No dream, sadly.'

How had she thought his voice smooth and delicious? It was so brusque now she almost felt it graze her skin.

That steady gaze was unnerving too. Why did he stare? Her head hurt but she'd been assured she'd feel better soon. Surely she didn't look that bad.

'Are you a doctor as well?'

The man's nostrils flared and his mouth thinned and she had the distinct impression he was annoyed. But why?

Unease trickled down her spine. He didn't move towards her yet she felt abruptly vulnerable.

The instinct was so strong she didn't hesitate. Gritting her teeth, she rolled a little to her side, lifting one leaden hand and planting it on the mattress, then struggling to push herself up.

Pain screeched through her. Her body was clumsy and uncoordinated but she kept going, drawing herself higher with slow determination till she was half sitting against the bed head, trembling with the effort.

When she looked at him again his arms were no longer folded across his chest but hung by his sides, his fingers clenching. A muscle in his jaw flexed and she sensed he reined in emotion. But why? What had she done?

If she could get off this bed she would, but her legs felt useless and she didn't want to end up in a heap on the floor. All she could do was cross her own arms protectively and meet that dark stare head-on.

'Who are you?' she whispered.

A noise escaped his throat. Something between a snort and a huff of disbelief.

'Really? That's the best you can do?'

She shook her head, bewildered, then stopped, wincing, as pain darted through her head then bounced around her skull. Her eyes flickered shut as she breathed through the hurt, willing it to subside.

When she looked again he was a step closer to the bed, a frown lining his forehead.

'I asked who you are.'

Her words were strident, tinged with sudden fear. Did he hear that in her voice? Possibly. For, instead of moving closer, he shoved his hands in his pockets and leaned back.

'You know exactly who I am. And I've got no time for this game of yours.'

'Game? You think this is a *game*?' Her voice rose as she lifted one hand towards her throbbing head.

The man's attention moved from her face to her raised hand, then down, past her mouth to her shoulder. Something about his stare made her look down.

She wore a fine cotton shirt, buttoned at the front and with the sleeves rolled up around her elbows. The shirt wasn't hers. She knew that from the way it swamped her, lying askew and revealing the whole of one shoulder.

For a second fear stabbed. Where were her clothes? Why wasn't she wearing her own things?

She thrust the questions aside and yanked the cotton up over her bare skin, clutching it closed at the neck. Her hands were unsteady and she refused to try tackling the buttons under this man's hawklike scrutiny.

'I assure you Mr... Mr Whatever Your Name Is, that this is no game.'

'I agree. There's nothing remotely amusing about it. So let's cut the pretence. Tell me what you're doing here.'

'I was injured. On the beach.'

That was what the doctor said, but she struggled to visualise it.

Something darted through her brain and her breath caught. But again, when she tried to hang onto it, it vanished into foggy nothingness.

'How were you injured?' His voice had a remorseless quality she hated. 'And on this particular beach?'

'I don't...' She paused, trying to still the strange, quivery feeling inside. 'Which beach was it? Where was I found?'

Anxiety nibbled at her, growing stronger by the second. The question wasn't just where she'd been but where she was now. And much more. There was so much that, she suddenly realised, she didn't understand. The strangely vague quality of her thoughts took on a new, sinister cast.

He rattled off a name in a foreign language. It was totally unfamiliar.

No, not totally. '*Isola?* That means island, doesn't it?'

He raised his hands and clapped, his expression mocking. The applause was deliberately slow, making heat flood her cheeks. '*Brava*. A fine performance. But not convincing enough. I know you, remember?'

She wanted to protest that she wasn't trying to convince him. That she didn't care what he thought. But she had bigger concerns. Finally her hazy brain clicked into gear and she understood the implications of what before had been only vaguely unsettling.

It hurt to swallow, as if sandpaper lined her throat. But that was a minor inconvenience. It was nothing compared with the huge, scary truth suddenly filling her brain. The truth she'd been too dazed to realise earlier.

'You know me?'

He rolled his eyes. 'Spare me the playacting. Of course I do.'

She gripped the shirt closer with fingers that had turned clammy as she fought rising panic.

'Then you can tell me who I am. Because I don't remember anything.'

CHAPTER TWO

ANGELO STARED DOWN at the woman before him, disbelief vying with fury.

Experience told him she was up to no good. Yet, despite what logic said, he found himself noting how vulnerable she looked.

There was more colour in her face than there'd been down on the beach. Then she'd looked pale as a corpse. Yet even now she conveyed an impression of fragility.

Those extraordinary eyes were wide and shadowed and a smattering of freckles on her nose and cheeks gave her an unexpectedly wholesome, almost naïve look. As if the sophisticate he'd known had turned into an innocent farm girl.

Angelo suppressed a bitter laugh at the idea.

Her hair, dark honey now rather than the pale gilt she'd once favoured, was dishevelled and naturally sexy. The woman he recalled had done everything she could to appear sleek and well-groomed at all times.

Rosetta had given her one of his shirts to wear. He recognised it as one he'd earmarked for charity donation. The material was fine, but it was huge on Alexa and he kept getting tantalising glimpses of her body, her breasts jiggling when she moved and sending a line of fire straight to his belly.

That, above all, amazed him. As he remembered it, he'd been totally impervious to her feminine allure when he'd discovered the truth about her.

'You don't remember anything?' he drawled. 'How very convenient.'

It seemed ridiculous, especially after all this time, that she could come back here. She must be desperate to try conning him again.

One thing was for sure—she'd picked the wrong man. He wasn't as gullible as he'd been half a decade ago.

'Actually,' she snapped, 'it's very *in*convenient.'

Her chin rose and her eyes blazed angrily.

Her anger surprised him.

Alexa had always known on which side her bread was buttered. She'd been all sweetness and light around him, right until the end. He'd discovered later that others, like his housekeeper, Rosetta, had borne the brunt of Alexa's displeasure when she didn't immediately get what she wanted. But with Angelo she'd been all smiles and acquiescence.

He watched as suddenly her mouth wobbled.

Because she'd realised belatedly that annoyance would win no sympathy?

Yet, despite his cynicism, Angelo's protective instincts surged. He'd looked after his widowed mother and younger sister all his adult life. He was, it was generally agreed, a *decent* man, kind to animals, children and those less lucky than himself. The sight of someone in distress, especially a woman, tugged at his conscience.

But this woman was the exception. 'Don't try that on me. If you want chivalry, you can look elsewhere.'

'Chivalry?' Her voice cracked. 'How about common courtesy?' She breathed deep as if trying to master her emotions and he had to force himself not to notice the way her nipples pressed against the thin shirt. 'Why can't you tell me your name and where we are?'

Angelo sighed and shrugged. 'I have no time or inclination for these games, Alexa.'

'Alexa?' Two vertical lines ploughed down between her eyebrows. 'Alexa?' she repeated more softly, as if trying out the sound of it.

Arrested, he paused, taken in despite himself, by the sight of her bewilderment. A shudder raked her and she closed her eyes, swallowing hard.

Suddenly she didn't look defiant or scheming but...forlorn.

Something sliced through him. A momentary doubt. A flash of sympathy and concern. But only for a moment.

When he'd met Alexa she'd been a moderately successful model with aspirations to act. She'd proved herself adept at playing a role around him and it had taken a sudden revelation for him to see through her charade. Clearly her skills had improved, if she could elicit even a moment's sympathy from a man who knew her for what she really was.

He turned on his heel. 'I don't have time for this.'

'Wait!' Lavender blue eyes held his and despite himself something softened within him. There'd been an edge to her voice that sounded like fear and, as he stared back, he registered that her breathing had turned quick and shallow.

'Alexa who?'

Angelo frowned. Did she still persist with this charade? 'Alexa Barrett,' he said finally, wondering what she hoped to achieve, pretending not to know.

Her lips moved and she silently repeated the name, as if committing it to memory. 'And we're in Italy.'

It wasn't a question but a statement, yet her

tone and knitted brow gave the impression she was perplexed.

'Southern Italy,' he murmured, leaning back and crossing his arms, curious, despite himself, to see what she'd do next. He couldn't figure what her plan was. His knowledge of Alexa told him she must have some scheme in mind to make her venture back here.

'The doctor.' Her gaze met his then skittered away. It was one of the few times he'd seen her discomfited and again it gave him pause. 'Will he come back soon?'

Angelo stared, trying to read her intentions in her features. But all he saw were hunched shoulders, the downward droop of her mouth and the fact that the hand grasping his shirt collar was white-knuckled.

He stifled automatic sympathy at the sight of a woman in distress.

'He'll come when he can. The weather's appalling and he had another emergency to see to. But he promised to return today.'

Angelo paused, his conscience grating. Whatever else was going on, Alexa *had* been unconscious when he'd reached her. That hadn't been a sham. The doctor had confirmed she'd had a knock to the head, advising that, for now, it was best she stay resting where she was.

Not what Angelo wanted!

But he couldn't throw an injured person out into the worst storm they'd seen in years. No matter how much he despised her.

'Is there something you need?'

That startled her. She actually jumped as if his words interrupted some deep reverie. Or as if she hadn't expected an offer of help.

Angelo's mouth firmed as guilt scored him. He didn't like this woman. Didn't trust her. But she'd been hurt and needed help.

'Water? Something to eat?' he persisted, watching her eyes widen and feeling annoyance rise. He wasn't an ogre. He was simply a man protecting his sanctuary.

She understood that. He wasn't the villain of the piece here.

'Thank you,' she said finally. 'Some water would be good.'

He nodded and strode to the bedside table, lifting the jug Rosetta had left and pouring some.

'Ah. Sorry. I didn't see it.' Alexa reached for the glass, carefully wrapping her fingers around the base of the glass as if intent on avoiding his touch.

Angelo's mouth curled. Who did she think she was trying to fool?

Then he swore under his breath as he released

the glass into her hold and realised too late that she was trembling. Water spilled and he only just caught the glass, and her hand, in his.

She was so unsteady it was hard to believe she faked it.

What did you expect? She was unconscious a few hours ago.

Silently Angelo cursed. He could at least have held his temper in check till a more appropriate time.

'Here.' He raised the glass to her lips, his hand cupping hers.

She drank greedily. This close, he became aware that the trembling wasn't just in her hand. Her whole body shook. Did she have a fever? He put the back of his hand to her brow and heard her swift intake of breath. An instant later she moved her head away. As if she didn't want to touch him any more than he wanted to touch her.

'That's enough, thanks.'

Angelo transferred the glass to the bedside table and topped it up again from the jug.

When he turned back she was sitting up against the antique carved headboard. It didn't look comfortable.

'Are you going to lie down again?'

Her glance ranged from him to the door and back before she answered. 'No, I'll sit up, thanks.'

Now that flash of energy had seeped away, she didn't look well. Angelo hoped the doctor would be back soon. He was getting concerned about his unwanted guest.

'Right.' He reached over to a couple of pillows discarded onto a nearby chair. 'Sit forward. You'll be more comfortable with these.'

Alexa moved, not forward but to one side, her movements slow and stiff, but it was enough to make space for the pillows behind her. When she sat back her breathing was fast and her milky pallor worried him.

'Thank you.' It was a barely audible husky sound. Yet she didn't look at him to see if she'd garnered sympathy. She stared across the room towards the view of the sea as if she'd never seen it before.

The fine hairs on Angelo's nape prickled to attention. He straightened and stepped back from the bed.

She didn't even glance in his direction. Not that he minded. Yet gut instinct stirred, telling him, as if he didn't know it, that something was wrong. Alexa had always been hyperaware of him, alert to any little change of mood or countenance. She'd read him like a book, a fact that had chagrined him when he'd discovered how she'd abused his trust.

But now he'd swear she was barely aware of his presence.

'Why are you here, Alexa?'

Slowly she turned her head. Her features were curiously blank. 'That's just it. I don't know. I don't remember.'

She saw his head rear back and his mouth draw in a straight, flat line.

Why was he so set on rejecting the truth? Why wouldn't he believe her?

To her horror, her mouth crumpled and she swung back to face the huge window. Emotion bubbled in her chest, making it tight and heavy with distress, a good match for her dully throbbing head.

She'd been so numbed by shock and pain before, and overwhelmed by the effort of answering the doctor's questions, that things hadn't sunk in. It was only now that she realised how small her world was, consisting merely of what she could see, touch, taste, hear and smell. Everything else was hidden by the misty nothingness that blurred her brain.

Her memory was a blank space. So blank it terrified her. Every time she groped for some snippet of the past it slid away.

She blinked and stared at the view of white-capped waves and lowering dark clouds billowing and scudding across the sky. The seascape was stunning, terrible yet strangely beautiful through the lashing rain.

Like the man standing beside the bed, silently seething. His impatience was like static prickling her skin and charging the air in the big, luxurious bedroom.

His stark disapproval matched the storm outside. As if he were a pagan weather god, living on a craggy hilltop, creating terrible storms when his mood turned sour.

If he smiled, would the sun come out?

She couldn't imagine that happening. He looked too dour. Besides, she suspected he'd be too dangerously attractive if he smiled.

She blinked, her thoughts circling back to her predicament. How could she distract herself with such absurd ideas when she was in a crisis?

Because it's easier than dwelling on the mess you're in. No memory. In a place you're clearly not wanted. With a man who loathes you.

She swallowed. Why should he loathe her? Maybe she was dreaming. All this, from the storm thundering outside to her companion who looked like the hero of some gothic romance, could be a nightmare.

'What are you doing?'

She sighed and released the skin of her forearm that she'd pinched between her fingers. 'Just checking I wasn't dreaming this.' She turned and met his dark gaze, relieved to find the banked anger had been replaced by curiosity. 'You're *sure* my name is Alexa?'

He nodded. 'Absolutely.'

She bit her lip, letting herself sink back against the pillows he'd provided. Sitting up straight had taken too much energy when every muscle felt as if it had been strung tight for too long.

'It doesn't sound familiar.' Panic stirred. 'Surely it should if I've answered to the name for...' Her breath caught on a hiccup.

'What is it?'

He wasn't exuding sympathy but there was no one else to help her and she needed, urgently, to understand what was happening.

Grimly she told herself this must be a temporary thing, caused by her accident. Yet that didn't stop fear eddying deep inside. What if this lack of memory was permanent? Was it possible?

'I don't even know how old I am.'

For a second she didn't think he'd respond. His face was set in stern lines as if he battled the impulse to walk away.

Cravenly she hoped he'd stay. Despite his attitude, he knew her. He could explain who she was and why she was here.

'You admitted to twenty-three when I knew you, but that was five years ago.'

He looked at her from beneath lowered brows in a stare that was part accusation and part restlessness. Stoically she ignored his mood, silently rejoicing in the fact she was in her twenties, not the several decades older she felt at this moment with her aching body and muzzy head.

'Admitted? There was some doubt?'

Why would she lie about her age?

He shrugged, the movement dragging her gaze across his emphatic shoulders and down to expressive hands that gestured dismissively. 'I learned to take everything you said with a pinch of salt.'

Did he mean she exaggerated? Or that she outright lied?

She swallowed hard. The picture he conjured was anything but flattering.

What had happened to make him hate her?

Perhaps it was stupid to feel upset about something she didn't recall, but who wanted their first snippets of self-knowledge to be so negative?

Surely this wasn't right.

Surely she wasn't the way he painted her.

As if you'd know. You don't even know your own name!

She let her eyes slide closed, wishing the headache would go. She didn't have the energy for these unpalatable glimpses into the past. Maybe if she slept again...

'Alexa.'

Her eyes snapped open. Eyes the colour of espresso coffee stared down at her, intent as if they could read her very soul.

It scared her that this man, this disapproving man, knew her better than she knew herself. And that he didn't trust her.

'I don't feel like an Alexa,' she blurted. 'It sounds...foreign.'

Slowly he straightened, his gaze still holding hers. For the first time she noticed a flicker of something that wasn't hard and judgemental there.

'On the beach you called yourself Ally.'

'Ally?'

Her lips formed the name, her tongue lingering clumsily on the sound. Did that sound any more familiar?

The answer was *no*. Nothing seemed familiar. Not even the sight of her ringless fingers and lightly tanned arms that she must have seen every day of her twenty something years.

'Yes. Short for Alexa, presumably.'

She put the heel of her hand to her breastbone, pressing down against the flutter of distress battering her chest. Any minute now she feared she might have a full-blown panic attack.

Her mind whirled. How did she know what a panic attack was when she didn't know anything about herself? It was totally bizarre.

'Don't worry about it now.' To her amazement his voice dropped again to that low, lush note that made her think of rich caramel and comforting warmth. 'Just shut your eyes and relax. The doctor will be here soon and someone will sit with you till he comes.'

She wanted to protest. To assert herself.

But to what end?

The last ten minutes had left her exhausted and wrung out. Talking and trying to think had taken all her strength.

She just hoped when she woke she'd be better.

With luck her memory would have returned. She'd enjoy proving to this disturbing, disapproving man that her name wasn't Alexa or Ally and that she wasn't the liar he believed her. She was someone else entirely. Of course she was.

Clutching that thought close, she felt her eyelids grow heavy and then the world went black.

* * *

Angelo kicked his heels in the hallway while the doctor examined Alexa.

She'd slept solidly for hours, sliding out of consciousness so abruptly it had startled him. One minute she'd been a curious mix of fire and fragility and the next she'd been out for the count. So deeply asleep, so still, that he'd worried she wasn't merely sleeping.

But when he'd put his fingers on the silky skin of her wrist he'd felt her even pulse. Nevertheless, every half hour or so he'd risen from the armchair beside her bed, where he'd dealt with a slew of business messages, to check she was breathing.

Obviously she had some self-serving reason for coming to his home. He suspected her supposed memory loss was a crafty ploy for sympathy. Yet she really *was* injured and a blow to the head could be dangerous. The doctor had been infuriatingly non-specific after his first visit, promising an update on his return.

Rosetta had offered to sit with Alexa but Angelo had rejected the idea. He, personally, would keep an eye on her.

Finally the doctor emerged and Angelo led the way downstairs to his study.

'A drink?'

The doctor shook his head, sinking into a

leather chair. 'Not with this storm still raging. I could be called out in the night. Now, about Ms Barrett...'

Angelo listened as the doctor talked at length about the woman ensconced in one of the guest suites. Listened with amazement.

'You mean it could be true? She could really have lost her memory?'

The other man frowned, his grave eyes piercing. 'You have some reason to suspect it's not true?'

Angelo paused. The doctor had only been on the island a few years, after Alexa's time here, and neither Angelo nor his staff had spoken about her since. As far as he knew there was no gossip about her on the island.

'I do. I knew her years ago. She wasn't trustworthy.'

'I see. But to fake amnesia...' He paused. 'It's possible. But that would be an extreme step.'

No more extreme than the lies Alexa had told before. The extreme lengths she'd gone to in order to get what she wanted.

'Amnesia isn't common but it's consistent with her injury.' The doctor paused. 'You mentioned that Ms Barrett understands Italian.'

'She does.'

'Fascinating. She appears not to understand

Italian now.' Did Angelo imagine an emphasis on the word *appears*? 'I must do some research and consult some colleagues.'

'Colleagues? Won't it be more efficient to move her to a mainland hospital?'

Then she'd be someone else's problem. Angelo suspected her convenient amnesia would probably dissipate then.

'No, no. That's not possible. Not with this weather. Did you hear about the chopper crash near Naples a few hours ago? Air ambulance is out and as for going by sea...'

The doctor looked towards the full-length windows. In the darkness beyond the wind screeched like the undead.

There'd be no sea crossing tonight or, if the forecast was correct, for a couple of days. This catastrophic storm, descending out of a clear spring day, was being described as one of the most destructive in living memory.

Which made him wonder again how Alexa had got to his private beach. No local would have brought her.

'She's best here, where she can rest quietly.' The doctor glanced around. 'It's good that you've got space to house her comfortably, and I'll come over regularly to check on her.'

'You want her to stay *here*?'

The other man's lips pursed. No doubt he thought Angelo was being uncharitable, not wanting to house an injured woman. But the doctor knew nothing of the woman's character. The thought of keeping her under his roof indefinitely...

'It's not ideal. But we must do the best we can in the circumstances.'

His stare hardened as if he expected Angelo to dispute that, but Angelo was a practical man. He understood that, for now there was no other option.

'Of course. She'll be well looked after.'

'I knew I could rely on you. Take heart, any memory loss is likely to be short-term. A few hours, maybe a few days.'

Unless she decided to spin it out, making the most of his charity.

But why? Angelo couldn't fathom what she hoped to gain.

The doctor reeled off a series of symptoms to look out for, in which case they should call him immediately. Then there were instructions about pain medication and the need for fluids.

Angelo listened carefully. Alexa Barrett would be well cared for. Hopefully she'd recuperate quickly and leave as soon as transport became available. Or sooner, if he could find alternative accommodation for her on the island.

Yet he had a deep-seated suspicion that it wouldn't be so easy to get rid of her.

Already she'd wormed her way back into his world, even his home.

The woman he'd vowed never to let near him again.

The woman who'd lied to him and betrayed him.

CHAPTER THREE

ALLY SAT IN an armchair near the window and stared at the boiling, dark sea.

After almost twenty-four hours she still had to make an effort to think of herself as Ally. But no other name had come to mind and it was better than Alexa, which just sounded wrong.

Or maybe it was the way her host said that name, as if repressing a sneer.

She shivered despite the warmth of the room and wished the rain would stop lashing the windows. Even to step out onto the balcony and draw a breath of salty sea air would be a relief.

All she'd seen was this bedroom and its adjoining bathroom. Partly because she didn't have the strength to go far with her weak knees and swimmy head, and partly because she hadn't been invited. She was here under sufferance.

Ally swallowed, forcing down the tangle of emotion that threatened to overwhelm her.

Everything will be all right. You just have to be patient.

She couldn't be claustrophobic. The suite was

spacious and comfortable, with panoramic views of the sea.

Yet she was uneasy, and not just because of her missing memory. At a deep-seated level Ally knew she didn't belong here.

What sort of house possessed a massive guest suite like this? Everything was the height of luxury. From the huge cloud-soft bed to the beautiful original artwork. From the massive sunken bathtub, complete with gorgeously scented jars of bath salts and oils, to the expensive marble gleaming white with the faintest delicate tracery of pale green.

She knew barely anything about herself but she sensed such opulence, even though tasteful and attractive, was alien to her.

The grounds visible from here reinforced the fact that this was no ordinary house. Despite the storm damage the gardens set high on the clifftop looked superb and the place commanded a spectacular view. She tried to imagine it on a sunny day.

Ally knew southern Italy was famed for its wide blue skies, stunning coastal towns and clear water. How she knew it, she couldn't say. Just as she couldn't understand how she knew that the sun rose in the east and set in the west, or that it was sensible to wear a broad-brimmed hat in the middle of summer.

Yet she still couldn't remember anything useful like her name or where she was from.

He'd said she was Australian and, as she clearly wasn't Italian, perhaps he was right. It was one of the few personal details her close-lipped host had let slip and she'd pounced on it gratefully.

Not that she trusted everything Angelo Ricci said. Far from it. He was biased against her for some reason.

Simply getting his name from him had felt like pulling teeth, one laborious tug at a time. Teeth from a particularly ferocious-looking wolf.

The man unnerved her with his brooding silences and judgemental attitude. As if she'd *asked* to be washed up on his precious beach!

From here she could see a sliver of pale sand on what Rosetta had explained was the private beach where she'd been found unconscious. Rosetta the housekeeper who, like her employer, didn't seem happy to have her here. She'd been polite, and the food she brought was delicious, but there'd been no generous smiles or warm welcome.

Ally frowned. She'd thought Italians were renowned for their hospitality. Or was that wishful thinking?

Her thoughts circled back inevitably.

How had she got there? Why was she alone? Surely someone, somewhere, missed her? She tried to imagine people frantically searching for her. A family, boyfriend, husband even.

A sob rose in her throat and she stifled it. She couldn't afford to give in to despair.

Doubtfully she looked down at her fingers. There was no ring and no mark from a ring. Her nails were neat and short. Nothing there to hint at her identity.

She lifted her hand to her head, then dropped it. The headache was bearable now, just a low hum, but she didn't want to make it worse by probing.

'What are you doing?' The words, sharp and unexpected, lassoed her ribs, tightening her lungs so her breath caught.

Cautiously, not wanting to aggravate the pain again, she turned.

Angelo Ricci stood just inside the open doorway. She hadn't heard him enter and he stood with his hands jammed onto his hips as if confronting some malefactor.

Ally stared straight back, refusing to be cowed when she'd done nothing wrong. 'Looking at the view.'

Surely that was evident. Yet that frown made him look as if he'd caught her stealing the family silver. Was that what he thought? That she'd come to ransack his home?

Was he going to tell her next that she was a thief as well as a liar? Ally braced herself.

'You shouldn't be out of bed.' He stalked across the room and she marvelled at the way those long legs ate up the space so quickly.

Another reminder of his sheer physicality. She'd been aware of it from the first and, despite her wariness—okay, her dislike of the man who so obviously disliked her—she kept noticing.

Her chin hiked up to keep him in view as he stopped before her. Despite pride and logic, and all her determination, it wasn't just dislike she felt.

Something stirred deep within. A frisson of sensation that she had no name for and was glad she didn't. Because the feeling was *soft* when she needed to be hard and on her guard around him.

'The doctor said I needed rest and quiet. I've been resting all day.'

Those black eyebrows crammed close and she was reminded again of some angry god, about to hurl a thunderbolt because his temper had got out of hand.

What would Angelo Ricci be like in a temper? Her pulse quickened but with excitement, not fear.

Was she a secret thrill-seeker? Or a blatant adrenaline junkie? What else could explain the sudden impulse to goad him?

Ally tamped it down. See? She was a sensible woman.

'What if you'd fallen? What if you'd hit your head again?'

Surprised, she searched his grim features. Was that concern in his voice? She dismissed the idea. He was probably worried that if she hurt herself again it would look bad, as if he'd failed to care for her.

'But I didn't. I was perfectly fine.'

Well, not perfectly. She'd been wobbly and wondered if she'd make it to the bathroom and back, but her need had been urgent and there'd been no one around to ask for help.

Ally's brow puckered as another thought surfaced. 'Did I dream it or did you stay with me through the night?'

She had vague memories of a dark, broad-shouldered presence in the shadows beyond the dimmed bedside lamp. Of firm hands supporting her as she sipped thirstily at a glass of water.

Ally had assumed it was a dream but, seeing the slight smudges beneath his dark eyes, she wondered. If so, it was an unexpected kindness.

He shrugged. 'Someone needed to keep an eye on you. Rosetta took the day shift.'

So she had. Not that Rosetta had stayed, but she'd looked in so often Ally began to wonder if that explained her dour attitude. The housekeeper would have plenty to do without checking on her every twenty minutes.

'Thank you. That's very kind.'

His eyes widened and she had the impression he was surprised. Because he didn't think she had the manners to thank him for his efforts? Or because he didn't usually do anything to elicit gratitude?

She wished she understood him. But not as much as she wished she understood herself.

Ally didn't like this man because he was abrasive and unfriendly. Because he knew things about her she didn't and seemed determined to look down on her.

Yet something inside her sparked into life when he was near. She felt a surge of energy and curiosity then. Strangely, despite everything, she felt safe.

Maybe she had some faint memory of him carrying her from the beach. The doctor had mentioned that and, having seen the steep drop to the beach, it made her appreciate Angelo Ricci's physical power and determination.

'What are you thinking about?'

Ally realised she was staring into that chiselled face as if she'd never seen a man before.

Suddenly she laughed. As far as her brain was concerned, she *hadn't*. Angelo Ricci and the nice doctor were the only men she could remember seeing.

Was that why he drew her gaze like a magnet?

Had she imprinted on him, like an orphaned duckling attaching itself to the first living being it encountered? The idea was ridiculous.

Yet awareness skittered through her, tightening her skin and beading her nipples. Ally snatched in a stifled gasp.

This couldn't be...*attraction*, could it? That was the last thing she needed.

Her laughter caught in something like a sob and she wrenched her head round towards the stormy sea.

What would be worse, discovering she really was attracted to this sour man? Or that her reaction was nothing special and she was easily attracted to any man?

Ally blinked as the backs of her eyes prickled.

She felt totally lost. Like a tiny rowing boat adrift on those monstrous waves outside. There was nothing to cling to. Nothing certain except this room, this man, and the fact that she wasn't welcome.

'Alexa—'

'Ally!' She sniffed. 'Please. I prefer it.' Though it still didn't feel like her real name.

Would she ever know what that was?

Despite the doctor's assurances she worried she might never recover her memory.

'Ally.' From her peripheral vision she saw Angelo Ricci hunker down beside her. 'What's wrong?'

A laugh escaped her tight throat. It was jagged and bitter and revealed too much but, beneath the stoicism she'd aimed for, her emotions ran too close to the surface.

'What's wrong? Apart from the fact I have no memory, I don't know who I am or how I got here. I don't know *anything*.'

Hearing her rising panic she snapped her mouth shut and looked away, transfixed by a single ray of light that beamed down through the roiling clouds. It illuminated a tiny disc of dark water, turning it to pewter. Yet as she watched the tiny gap closed, the clouds bunching together, and everything turned dark again.

Would the clouds of confusion in her brain ever pull back enough for her to remember the past? Ally looked down to find her hands clenched in the long tails of the fine cotton shirt covering her thighs.

His shirt? Probably. The idea spilled heat into her cheeks and across her breasts. Suddenly she was hyper-conscious that she wore nothing beneath the oversized shirt she'd been using as a nightie. She smoothed it down her thighs then hitched the open collar high at her throat.

'The doctor is convinced you'll get your memory back. You just have to give it time.'

Angelo grabbed the other armchair near the window, turning it to face her rather than the balcony. An instant later he was blocking her view, sitting right in her line of sight.

'What if he's wrong? What if it never returns?'

He spread his hands in a gesture that spoke of patience and acceptance. Qualities that felt elusive right now.

'We cross that bridge when we come to it.'

'We?' She frowned. 'There's no *we*. Just me.'

His eyes held hers. Dark brown eyes that looked impenetrable and at the same time full of a knowledge she could barely guess at. She looked for sympathy. What she saw, or thought she saw, was wariness.

It made her push back in her chair.

He didn't *want* to sympathise, she realised. For

some reason he was determined to keep her at arm's length.

'You'll be okay—'

'Don't let me keep you,' she said, maintaining an even tone despite the whirlpool of despair and fear threatening to suck her under. 'I've already taken up enough of your time.' She paused, searching for something else to hurry him on his way. 'You're right. Of course I'll be okay.'

Angelo looked her in the eye and tried to convince himself she was right. That she didn't need his help.

Because she had to be faking this so-convenient amnesia. He understood she'd had some sort of accident but she could only have come here as part of a deliberate scheme. To win his sympathy so he'd take her back?

Surely even Alexa couldn't believe that. Nothing on this earth would make him welcome her into his life. Logic told him she'd capitalised on circumstances to elicit his sympathy and let her stay. The storm had played into her hands. His island retreat was just that, a retreat. It wasn't the sort of place she'd visit on her way somewhere else. Which meant she'd sought him out.

Yet, seeing the anxiety in her shadowed eyes,

the frown pleating her forehead and the nervous way she chewed the corner of her mouth, Angelo felt a tendril of doubt. He tried to recall her doing that in the past and failed. It was a new thing. Maybe a deliberate tactic.

He knew her acting skills of old, which was why he couldn't trust this woman. And yet…

Did he imagine that her face was slightly more rounded than he remembered? She *was* the same woman, wasn't she? Of course she was. Apart from her looks and voice, that eye colour was unique.

She looked away, fumbling to do up the top button of his shirt.

There it was again. Another reaction from her that didn't fit expectations. The Alexa he'd known had been proud of her body and loved to flaunt it. She'd thrived on male adulation, even when she was supposed to be in a committed relationship.

Was it possible she wasn't faking the amnesia?

It would take more than that to convince him.

'Alexa… Ally.' Angelo made his tone easy, gentle even. As if he had no suspicions about her motives. He'd treat her as what she ostensibly was, a chance met visitor. He'd give her sanctuary then send her on her way. 'You're safe here.

The doctor expects you to begin regaining your memory soon. When that happens I'll help you get back to where you belong.'

Which, thankfully, was far from here.

Angelo ignored the traitorous little jab of heat to his belly as she stirred, her shapely legs sliding against each other as she tucked them further under the chair. Ostensibly the move was decorous, hiding some of her bare skin. In reality it reminded him of the fact she was clearly naked beneath his shirt. A fact he refused to dwell on.

'Thank you. I'm sure that will be a relief for you.'

'And for you,' he said easily. 'I can't imagine what it must be like, unable to remember anything.'

Her chin lifted in a movement that was suddenly completely familiar. Relief trickled through him. Occasionally, despite logic, Angelo found himself wondering if he was mistaken about his uninvited guest. But that movement was pure Alexa. Once upon a time he'd found it endearing. Later it had presaged obstinacy.

'It's unpleasant in the extreme.' Then, just as abruptly, the fight left her and her shoulders slumped. 'You know my name. Surely you can tell me more?'

'I have no idea what you were doing here. I

hadn't seen you for a very long time and I never expected to see you again.'

That was the way Angelo preferred it.

He watched her head rear back as she digested the finality in his tone. Good. If she thought by staying here she might worm her way onto his good side, the sooner she realised her mistake the better.

'But you know more, don't you? Anything you can tell me will help.'

She wrapped her arms around her middle, leaning towards him as if hanging on anything he might contribute. As if she didn't notice the way the gesture pulled his shirt across her breasts, revealing tight nipples and surprisingly lush curves.

Angelo breathed out slowly and told himself he was too canny to be taken in by the obvious ploy.

He'd play her game, for now. She was injured and there was nowhere for her to go on this privately held island. No hotels. Not even guesthouses. The locals, whether born and bred here over generations, or rich incomers who'd bought into the exclusive location as an escape from the rat race, valued privacy.

'You're Australian.' She nodded, her bright eyes fixed on his. 'When I met you you'd been in Europe for a while, modelling. Not top-of-the-range couture collections but sportswear, swim-wear and lingerie.'

Something flickered across her face and her mouth turned down a little. Maybe she wasn't pleased at being reminded she hadn't hit the heights she'd aspired to.

'And my family? Where in Australia did I come from?'

Angelo shook his head. 'No idea. You never mentioned where you came from and said you had no close family.'

She'd been close-mouthed about both, airily saying she had no ties and no wish to live in the past. But she'd later mentioned her parents were dead and she was an only child.

In the early days he'd suspected some family tragedy, for he'd caught a flash of what looked like pain in her expression, so he hadn't pushed for details. After all, he knew how deep pain could run, losing his father too early.

'I see. What else? Where did I live?'

'You shared a flat in Rome but you gave it up. There was some disagreement with your flat-mate.'

'Was she another model? Do you know her name? Maybe I can trace her.'

Angelo shook his head. Was Alexa really going to persist with this charade?

What if it's not a charade? What if she really has lost her memory?

The idea unsettled him. He didn't want to feel sympathy for this woman who'd barged through his life like a wrecking ball. Even now he was itching to get up and leave. It took all his control to maintain a polite façade. But he'd promised the doctor he'd look after her. Angelo would do whatever it took to get her physically mended so she could go and never come back.

'No idea. But your flatmate wasn't a woman. He was your lover.'

Her eyes widened and her mouth sagged and, if he didn't know better, he'd think he'd shocked her.

As if she couldn't imagine herself with a man. The irony pulled his lips into a grimace.

'My lover?'

'*Ex*-lover. You moved out. Took all your things.'

'I see.'

She nibbled her bottom lip again and Angelo felt his groin tighten. Did she know the action drew attention to the sweet shape of her mouth? It was one of the things he'd first noticed about her. That and the beckoning light in her stunning eyes.

And her body, lithe and seductive.

Despite himself, Angelo's attention dropped to

her breasts, straining against his shirt. There was something disquieting about the fact it was *his* shirt she wore against her skin. The knowledge elicited an all too familiar tension in his belly. Sexual tension that had once led him to drop his guard, with calamitous consequences.

His gaze skimmed the indent of her waist, accentuated by her folded arms.

Alexa had changed since he'd seen her. She'd gained weight, her feminine curves more pronounced, though she was still slender.

Shocked at the direction of his thoughts, he snapped his gaze up, but she hadn't noticed his lapse. That, in itself, gave him pause. Once Alexa had been totally attuned to every nuance of his expression, voice and body. She'd studied him and learned to anticipate his desires.

Angelo sat straighter, resolution starching his spine.

Swiftly he catalogued the other changes in her.

She looked as young and fresh-faced as she had five years ago. But she did her hair differently, not sleek but loose and casual around her shoulders. It was a different shade too, dark honey instead of pale gilt, and there was a sprinkling of freckles across her face. He didn't remember those before.

She pushed a hand through her hair and he noticed her nails, short and unvarnished. So different to the long nails she'd once favoured, their colour changing to complement each new, expensive outfit.

She moved and suddenly Angelo found himself staring into wide eyes that were an impossible, entrancing shade of blue verging into purple. A shade he'd seen in no one but her.

His pulse thudded. She was a stunning woman despite her character flaws.

Which proved you couldn't judge on appearances.

'How do we know each other, Angelo?'

His attention caught on the way she said his name. Alexa had always prided herself on her perfect Italian accent. Now she said his name slightly differently. But then she was pretending she didn't speak Italian.

Or was that real, not pretence?

Either way it was far too confronting having her in his home. Deep-seated emotions bombarded him. Shame, regret and self-disgust at how he'd let her dupe him, and through him the people he loved.

He'd promised his dying father that he'd care for and protect his mother and sister, but he'd failed them and his *papà*. He'd broken that sacred trust when he'd allowed this woman to hurt them. His gut clenched as he fought nausea at how he'd let them all down.

'You need to rest.' His voice was rough. 'We'll continue this later when you're stronger.'

'No!' No weakness in her now. She was all determination. '*Tell* me. Did we know each other well?'

He folded his arms and looked her in the eye. He'd had enough.

'In some ways we knew each other as well as any two people can.' Her eyes rounded in a display of shock that made him want to smash through her ridiculous pretence.

'You were my mistress. Then you were my wife.'

CHAPTER FOUR

ALLY STARED AT the man before her, the man with cold eyes and a grimace on his lips, and felt her gorge rise. The fine hairs along her arms lifted and her nape tightened.

You were my mistress. Then you were my wife.

His tone was dismissive. As if she had no place in the world except in relation to Angelo Ricci.

Through her nausea, bitter amusement surfaced. That was still the case. With her memory gone, reliant on this man, she literally didn't have a life beyond the boundaries of his home.

A wave of terror crashed through her and she gritted her teeth, fighting down distress.

The inimical light in those dark eyes told her he'd been deliberately brutal. That was enough to make her harness what strength she possessed to stare him down.

Did something shift in his expression? Some flicker of emotion?

The very thought seemed inconceivable.

'Your *wife*?'

The word pulled a thread of heat down from

her breasts to her belly and lower, to a feminine place that suddenly felt alive.

'Yes.'

'Are we still married?'

The abrupt sideways jerk of his head was eloquent enough, but he made it totally clear. 'Divorced.'

Every syllable dripped disdain.

For her? Or for the fact they'd divorced? Yet looking into those set features she couldn't believe he regretted ending their marriage. He looked anything but lover-like.

Her mouth thinned. 'Is that all you have to say?'

He shrugged. 'Isn't that enough?'

He was right. It was more than enough. Ally sank back in her chair, head spinning and heart thudding.

She had no memory of this man, despite the feeling, once or twice, that she'd seen his face before. Surely if they'd been intimate, she'd remember something?

Her cheeks burned at the thought of being his mistress. What did that entail? Sex on demand, pandering to his every whim? Fire swirled in her belly and she shifted on the padded seat.

Ally tried to imagine wearing glamorous

gowns and jewellery, accompanying him to glittering parties. Tried and failed.

Or maybe—the thought made her insides churn—she'd been the sort of mistress to wear thigh-high leather boots and wield a whip.

Except one glance at that proud, stern face assured her that was unlikely. Angelo Ricci didn't look the sort of man to cede power to anyone.

Her head spun. The thought of being intimate with Angelo Ricci unnerved her. Her gaze drifted from the stark male beauty of that disapproving face to wide shoulders and a powerful torso that even now, despite his attitude, made her wish for things she shouldn't. Even his long-fingered hands looked capable and uncompromisingly masculine. As for those strong legs with their bunched thigh muscles straining the denim of his jeans…

Ally gulped as she felt a melting sensation between her legs. Something quivered into life deep inside.

She'd told herself she couldn't imagine herself with this dour man. Yet really she could imagine it too easily. Could almost feel the brush of warm denim and hard muscle beneath the pads of her fingers. Her hands tickled at the thought of touching the olive skin of his forearms with their smattering of dark hair.

As for touching him elsewhere, and being touched by him…

She looked up abruptly and met his eyes. That angry expression was gone, replaced by an expression that made her blood sizzle in her veins. Those dark eyes glittered, alive with something that might have been hunger. Something heated and primal.

Except the next instant it had gone, leaving her feeling…bereft.

His unreadable stare made it clear she'd imagined that momentary blast of longing. Which was all too believable given her malfunctioning mind.

Ally chewed her lip, fighting to get her brain working again. She told herself any fancied attraction to Angelo Ricci was a product of that knock to her head. It couldn't be real.

'You said I was your mistress.' She paused, hating the sourness on her tongue that the word invoked. She had to push herself to get the words out. 'Are you saying you were married before to someone else and I was…with you then?'

His head reared back and the look he gave her was full of disdain. 'Of course not. I'm an honourable man. I'd never break my vows and cheat on my wife.'

Ally's shoulders slumped in relief. The thought

of being the other woman in some love triangle was abhorrent. 'So when you say *mistress*…?'

His nostrils flared, emphasising the finely chiselled shape of his nose. 'Maybe you prefer *kept woman*?'

No, she didn't. She hated it.

He implied she'd *sold* herself to him for money. What about her self-respect? Ally couldn't imagine doing anything so venal.

On the other hand, who was she to say what she would have done? She had no memory. Only an instinctive distress at the idea of being any man's paid sexual partner.

What did that mean? Was her mind playing tricks? Was the sensation that this was all wrong, that she couldn't have done any of this, a subconscious effort at avoidance?

'I see.' Then on a burst of anger she blurted, 'Your word choice says a lot about you.'

He raised his eyebrows in query. 'You think?'

Ally nodded. 'It's deliberately demeaning. You could have said *girlfriend, partner* or *lover*. Instead you chose to be insulting.'

Maybe she'd been an English teacher, spending her days finding meaning in the written word. Or maybe she was simply a woman not used to being insulted and dismissed. Either way, she was grateful for the flash of anger that strengthened her sinews.

She arched her own eyebrows and met his stare, noticing the flex of his jaw and the quick flick of his pulse, as if her needling had struck home. Good.

'You're right.' He nodded stiffly, his discomfort obvious. 'I'd never describe any other lover as my mistress. I've let our history colour my word choice.'

Her skin tightened. She wasn't looking forward to hearing this, but she had to know. 'Go on.'

'We lived together in what we agreed would be a short affair. You preferred to live in luxury at my expense than work, which *did* make you different to my previous lovers. I paid your way and you were particularly pleased when I bought you gifts.'

His tone suggested those gifts were expensive. Ally's stomach dived. The more she discovered about her past, the more she wished it all a bad dream.

She brushed her hands up and down her arms, trying to stimulate blood flow to counteract the chill engulfing her. It was on the tip of her tongue to observe that maybe paying for a woman's companionship was the only way Angelo Ricci could get one to stay.

But he'd just laugh. Even when he looked down his nose at her, he was still a man who drew the eye.

Drew the eye! He was magnificent, dangerous and brooding. He'd attract women like moths to a flame. Until they discovered there was nothing soft or caring beneath that adamantine exterior.

Ally shuddered. 'Thank goodness that's over.'

Dark eyes narrowed on her as if he didn't believe she'd said that.

Let him think what he liked. She had more on her mind than whether Angelo Ricci was happy.

'Yet we married. Surely that means we were in love once?'

'Love?' His deep voice hit a jarring note that grated through her. 'Hardly. You married me for my money.'

It was like a slap to the face. She flinched, absorbing the shock. Yet another shock. When would they end?

His eyes glinted with pure dislike and, finally, Ally understood. That was why he didn't want her here. That was why he was so unfriendly and his housekeeper refused to smile. He thought her a gold-digger who'd tried to take advantage of him.

Ally was torn between disbelief, because that couldn't be who she was, and an absurd desire to say she was sorry. But apologising for something she didn't remember? That meant accepting his words at face value. Surely it took two to break a marriage, just as there were two sides to every story. She was hearing his version of events. What was hers?

She blinked and stared down at her hands, now clasped in her lap. Her head was throbbing again and the edges of her vision blurred. When she moved too fast she felt giddy. But she couldn't stop now. She had to know everything.

'If I was avaricious, why marry me?'

Her ex-husband shot to his feet.

Ex-husband. She still found it incredible.

He swung around to face the window and shoved his hands in the front pockets of his jeans. Ally's gaze caught on the tight curve of his backside in faded denim.

Suddenly the notion of them being together, being intimate, wasn't so difficult to believe. Her throat dried and she swallowed hard.

'It was a mistake. One I regretted almost immediately.'

She opened her mouth then closed it again.

What did it matter now? Did she really want to trawl through every last detail of something that had obviously ended acrimoniously?

She longed for something positive. To hear just

one thing about herself that she could build on. To hear of one good quality she had. But she wouldn't get that here.

So far her skills were sex and spending money! If she'd kept this man, who exuded sexual chemistry, happy in bed, happy enough to promote her from mistress to wife, she must be very good at sex.

Ally grimaced and propped her head in her hands.

That *wasn't* what she was hoping for.

Was it totally naïve to think that somewhere in the world she had friends and family who liked her, missed her and worried why she wasn't in contact?

Was it weak to hope that someone cared about her? That she wasn't the black-hearted opportunist he painted?

A day later Angelo hunched against the buffeting wind, prowling the strip of beach that had narrowed with the high seas. The storm's fury had eased briefly and he needed fresh air. Being cooped up in the house with his ex-wife made him feel hemmed in. Even though he only saw her to check she was all right.

She was visibly improving, so hopefully she

wouldn't be here long. But that still left the question of why she'd returned.

He kicked a pebble across the pale pink sand, listening to the slap of waves and the roar of the wind.

It was more than claustrophobia he suffered. His feelings were an uncomfortable mix of suspicion, fascination, doubt and guilt.

Suspicion because he knew her too well. He'd be crazy to believe her tale of accidentally washing up on his beach.

Fascination—his breath snagged—*that* was unexpected. Every time he was with her he was aware of her femininity, her feistiness and stoicism, completely at odds with the hatred he'd harboured for years. He admired her spirit and, more worryingly, the curl of her mouth when she smiled unexpectedly or the sound of her voice with its familiar accent that somehow wasn't quite the voice he recalled. As for his response to her flagrantly feminine and alluring body… no, better not to think of that.

Doubt. Now that was a surprise. Because, despite his well-grounded suspicion, he'd begun to wonder if, whatever her original scheme, she really had lost her memory.

She'd asked how he knew her and he'd told her. Then watched the colour flare in her cheeks before receding. Surely that wasn't an act. Her eyes had darkened, pupils too big against those vivid irises. He'd read stress in her restless hands and tense jaw and despite himself he'd felt pity. Perhaps this really was all new to her. He wouldn't bet money on it. Nothing would convince him to trust Alexa again, but maybe he'd been unnecessarily harsh. Certainly he had been if she truly suffered from amnesia.

Which led to guilt. Because he hadn't been gentle or conciliatory but driven by emotion. He'd made no allowance for the fact she was injured and that shamed him.

It wasn't enough to admit that he hated being reminded of their past. Of how easily she'd played him. Their fiasco of a marriage was as much his fault as hers. Because he should have known better.

He had a reputation for clear thinking. For cutting through complex situations. It had helped him turn the family's bank into an international powerhouse. It had helped him support his mother and sister, taking on the mantle of head of the family before his time. Yet still Alexa had deceived him spectacularly. And that had had awful consequences for those he loved.

Setting his jaw, Angelo clambered onto the rock platform at the end of the beach and looked out to sea. Even in this weather it was spectacular, his private slice of heaven.

He turned to go and paused, noticing something wedged in a crevice. A flash of yellow and aqua. Curious, he climbed down and retrieved it.

It was a long paddle designed for use with a stand-up paddleboard. The logo of a hire store on the mainland was emblazoned on it, a place that rented jet skis and windsurfers to tourists. There was a chunk out of the blade and a crack up to the haft. Not surprising if it had been adrift during the storm.

Or involved in an accident.

The hairs on Angelo's nape stood on end as he wondered what accident might cause such damage.

He thought back to the afternoon before last. To the speedboat racing too close to shore. If someone had been swimming off the beach, or balancing on a paddleboard when it rounded the point...

Surely the boat would have stopped. Unless they hadn't realised there'd been an accident. If Alexa had been coming in to shore and lost her balance in the wake of the boat she could have knocked her head on a submerged rock.

Angelo's blood chilled. It was feasible. If true, she was lucky to be alive.

He spent another half-hour combing the rocks at either end of the beach for signs of a paddleboard, or other detritus. Finally the worsening weather forced him back up the cliff, paddle in hand.

Was that how Alexa had reached the island? She'd have to be proficient to do it and he'd never thought of her as athletic. On the other hand, she'd proved herself capable of anything in pursuit of her goals. Only someone reckless or utterly determined would make for the island with a storm bearing down.

Ten minutes later he was speaking to the owner of the marine rental shop. Yes, they were missing a paddleboard. They'd raised the alarm for a missing tourist but emergency services had been so busy on the coast there'd been no news yet.

No, they didn't have a name for the woman. The owner confirmed it *was* a young woman, his tone proof that she'd been attractive.

She'd rented a locker for her belongings while she was out on the water, but it had revealed nothing useful. They'd opened it to search for evidence of her identity when she hadn't returned. But, unlike every other tourist, she had no luggage or identification with her. There'd been a bag with water, a change of clothes, sun cream and some cash. No credit card, no passport. Not

even a hotel room key. Nothing to show her name
or where she was staying.

As if she didn't want to be identified.

The thought took hold as the other man ex-
pounded on how strange it was that she'd travelled so light. To Angelo, who knew the lengths
Alexa would go to in order to get what she
wanted, it confirmed his suspicions.

Amnesia or not, his ex was up to no good.

Angelo knocked on the door to her suite but got
no answer. He waited and tried again.

'Alexa?' Silence. Yet she couldn't be asleep.
Rosetta had spoken with her mere minutes earlier, sitting by the window. He knocked again,
concern rising. Had something happened to her?
Some medical complication? 'Alexa?'

Turning the handle, he stepped inside. The bedside lamp was on against the afternoon gloom
but there was no sign of Alexa. His gaze swung
towards the bathroom door as it opened.

A waft of fragrant air preceded her. His nostrils twitched as the scent of neroli reached him,
rich and citrusy. Then she was in the doorway,
wet hair combed back from her face, her feet
bare and body covered past the knees in a white
towelling bathrobe.

'You!' She faltered on the threshold, eyes rounding.

As if he didn't have a right to be in his own home. He ignored the fact he'd never normally walk into a guest's suite uninvited, especially a female guest's.

Angelo was about to say he'd worried something had happened to her but stopped himself. Better not to let her know of his concern. The woman he'd known would see that as weakness and twist it to her advantage.

'We need to talk.'

She smoothed back her hair in a gesture that might have signalled vulnerability if it weren't for those flashing eyes and the challenging upward hike of her chin.

'Unless you're in pain. If you need rest…'

See, he could be reasonable.

'I'm fine.'

She stepped into the room and Angelo silently agreed. She looked very fine indeed. Even wrapped in that bulky robe, Alexa was more alluring than he could recall her ever being in a minuscule bikini or lacy lingerie.

Was his mind playing tricks?

Maybe it was the wholesome look that appealed, a contrast to the subtle yet ever-present make-up she'd previously worn. Alexa had always looked polished, prepared for male adulation. At first he'd enjoyed the fact she made an effort to appear her best at all times. Till he realised how fixated she was on her appearance and that there was something lacking beneath her pretty façade. She ruthlessly wielded her looks and femininity like twin blades, determined to win what she wanted at all costs.

Now, with her face bare, she looked stunningly sexy and natural. Her eyelashes were spiked and her cheeks and throat flushed as if she'd been in a hot shower just moments ago. That idea was reinforced as he watched a single drip of water slide down her jaw.

Instantly Angelo had a vision of her naked in the shower. Of water cascading lovingly over the lush body he'd caught glimpses of the last couple of days through one or other of his shirts.

It was *that* intimacy, he decided, the fact she'd been naked but for clothes he'd once worn, that skewed his thinking down this unwanted path.

'Perhaps you'd like to sit.' He gestured to the armchairs near the window.

Instead of accepting his invitation she shook her head. Far from looking weak, she appeared energised. 'I'd rather you told me what you want then leave.'

Her voice was as sharp as a slap to the cheek.

Angelo's jaw clamped but he bit back a retort. It didn't matter if she accepted his olive branch. Still, her response rankled.

'I want to discuss how you got here.'

Her eyes narrowed, fire glinting there as surely as if ignited with a match. It intrigued Angelo. Alexa had always previously hidden her emotions.

'I told you I don't remember. What part of that don't you understand?'

His eyebrows shot up. It was unlike Alexa to show aggression. 'Actually, I have information to share with *you.*'

He folded his arms and watched her frown. She raised a hand and raked a hand back through her hair again. Did he imagine she suddenly looked fragile?

Maybe. Or maybe she was scared he'd discovered something she didn't want uncovered.

'I'm sorry. I shouldn't have snapped. I'm a bit...' She gestured vaguely. 'I'm not at my best.'

Angelo surveyed her for a moment then nodded. 'I understand.'

Strangely, he did. He didn't trust her but if she'd lost her memory totally...

'What have you got to tell me?'

* * *

Maybe he had news that would stir recollections.

'I think I know how you got here.'

Ally shoved her hands into the robe's pockets and tried to find her equilibrium. The way he looked at her told her to prepare for some new blow.

What could be worse than yesterday's revelations? She still couldn't get her head around them.

Then there was Angelo's patent dislike. It made her feel tainted and ashamed that anyone should dislike her so much. At the same time she resented his brutal way of sharing their past. As if he'd enjoyed shocking her.

Ally straightened her spine. At least she'd regained her physical strength, despite some bruising and her scarily blank mind.

Yet she wasn't as confident as she tried to appear while she waited for him to continue. Cooped up in these rooms with no distraction from her thoughts was driving her crazy, leaving her emotions askew.

That had to explain her reaction when she'd seen Angelo in the doorway, looking from the bed to her. Something hot and needy had flared inside. There'd been a gleam in his eyes that spoke of awareness and for an instant she'd felt an answering flash of desire. She assumed it was desire. A dragging weight low in her body and a softening between her thighs.

How could she respond sexually to a man who despised her? Did she have no pride? No self-control?

Ally thought of the picture he'd painted of her and wondered if perhaps she didn't.

Suddenly she wished she'd taken the chair he'd offered. Her brain was whizzing and adrenaline shot around her body, making her poised for flight. Or fight.

And how it was she recognised that, when she didn't recognise her name, she had no idea.

'You came by sea. I've checked locally and there are no reports of a missing foreigner.'

'Go on.' There had to be more. It had always seemed obvious she'd come ashore at his beach.

'I found a paddle in the rocks at the end of the beach. The sort used with stand-up paddle-boards.'

Dark eyes narrowed on her as if watching for some infinitesimal reaction. What did he expect? A flash of memory? Her lips tightened. If only...

'You think I paddled from the mainland?'

Her gaze shot to the glass doors onto the balcony where she'd caught a smudge of darkness earlier that might be the mainland. But the weather had closed in again and all she saw was thrashing rain and greyness. But his words jogged no memory. Ally breathed deep, trying to stifle disappointment.

'It's a fair distance but doable for someone fit enough.' His gaze flickered over her, as if assessing her physical fitness, and Ally's skin prickled. It wasn't a sexual look yet she felt hyper-sensitive to his scrutiny.

'Okay.' She made herself focus. 'If that's the case then I was staying on the mainland. If we search—'

'Already done.' His gaze turned laser sharp, making Ally wish she wore something more than the plush robe against her bare skin. 'I traced the guy who rented out a paddleboard for cash to a woman who meets your description. He'd already reported you missing to the authorities.'

Ally caught her breath, her hand going to her throat as anticipation swelled. This felt like progress at last. 'They've traced where I was staying?'

Surely, once she returned there and was reunited with her belongings, it would jog her memory.

Eagerly, she moved closer, only stopping when she caught a delicious hint of male scent, warm skin, citrus and cedarwood and realised what she'd done. She was a mere arm's length from the man who might be her host yet felt like her enemy.

Ally planted her feet on the antique carpet, refusing to back away. She wouldn't be cowed by him.

She breathed deep, telling herself she was intrigued to be able to identify the components of the scent, including a hint of pepper. This *wasn't* a response to him as an attractive man. It was her discovering more about herself.

Maybe she was a perfumer? Or worked in a department store, selling expensive colognes? Excitement stirred.

'Now that's the interesting thing, Alexa. There was no trace of a missing stranger staying locally. Your name on the rental book was an unreadable scrawl too, though it started with an A. They checked the locker where you left your belongings but there was nothing to identify you. Just a set of clothes and cash.'

'Ally. I told you I don't like being called Alexa.' Which was probably why he did it. 'What about a hotel key?'

Angelo shook his head. 'Nothing. It's as if you didn't want to be traceable. As if you carefully planned it that way because you were scheming something.'

She frowned, her mind working furiously. 'That's far-fetched, don't you think?'

He spread his hands, shrugging his shoulders. 'Nothing would surprise me.'

With you. He didn't say it but he didn't need to.

It was merely one more provocation on top of the others—his snarkiness as he'd described their previous relationship, his housekeeper's air of acting under sufferance, the lack of warmth from anyone except the doctor. On top of the terrible clawing fear that maybe she'd never regain her memory, it was too much.

Ally stepped forward right into his personal space, and poked him in the chest.

A surge of power filled her as she saw his eyes widen. It felt wonderful to take the initiative for a change.

'You're unbelievable! Do you know that? I'm the *victim* here but still you can't accept it.'

She pushed again into that hard chest, wishing she could shove him back, or make him feel some of the pain she'd experienced.

She wanted…she didn't know what she wanted precisely, but letting her emotions off the leash felt glorious.

'So what if I didn't leave a credit card in a locker? That's not a crime. And it's not proof of a conspiracy. Or are you so totally caught up in

your own importance you think the world re-
volves around *you*? That the only reason I could
possibly visit the area is because of you?'

She was panting, her breath coming in sharp
tugs, but she didn't care. She looked into those
liquid dark eyes and some devil urged her on.
For the first time she felt alive and full of sparkling certainty instead of inhabiting a shadowy
half-life.

'For all you know I was visiting a friend here.'

'No one has come forward to report their friend
missing.'

Ally rolled her eyes. 'Maybe I rented a villa.
Maybe I came here for sun, sea and relaxation.
Maybe I didn't even think about the possibility
you'd be here. Did you think of that?'

'Impossible.' Long fingers closed around hers,
flattening them against his chest to stop her prod-
ding.

Ally frowned, registering a heavy thud and realising it must be the beat of his heart.

'Why is it impossible?'

His mouth caught at the corner in a grimace
and when he spoke it was in a whisper that
scraped across her bones. 'Because of this.'

Then his head lowered and his mouth took hers.

CHAPTER FIVE

THERE WAS A moment when she could have pulled back or pushed him away. But she didn't.

Because she didn't want to.

The knowledge hit her as warm lips covered hers implacably yet with something curiously like gentleness. This was no hard mashing of teeth against lips.

This didn't feel predatory or like domination.

It felt…perfect, she realised as her eyes shut and her mouth opened and she leaned into him as if this was what she'd wanted all along.

Maybe it was.

The thought shivered through her.

Maybe the jittery uncertainty and the way she'd baited him were because she needed to discover what it felt like, being kissed by Angelo Ricci.

Held by him, for now his arms roped around her, hauling her close so she felt his solid heat all down her front. Every bit of him felt unforgiving, pure muscle and bone, and utterly spellbinding.

Or maybe that was because he worked magic on her.

Who'd have thought the thin-lipped mouth that

had looked sardonic and disapproving could feel so wonderful?

Ally sighed and arched her neck as she leaned closer, cataloguing the rich taste of coffee and potent male. It was heady, addictive.

Did she subconsciously remember and crave physical contact with Angelo?

She should be horrified or at least embarrassed.

She wasn't. Instead she wallowed in sensation. The contrast of his hard maleness against her own body, which felt suddenly melting and soft. The taste of him as his tongue danced and slid against hers. The tang of his scent in her nostrils, the heavy pound of his throbbing heart beneath her now splayed hands. The easy, yet thorough way his mouth seduced hers.

Were kisses always like this?

Ally's head spun as she tried and failed to grasp at a comparison. She had none. To all intents and purposes this was her first kiss. She recalled none that had gone before, not even a hint of memory.

Surely she'd have remembered something so wonderful?

If kissing Angelo was like this, what would it be like to make love with him?

His hand caressed her cheek, cupping her jaw and angling her head for better access. Abruptly she lost her train of thought as she eddied into a whirlpool of bliss.

Her hands crept up his powerful chest and circled around his neck. His hair was short at the back, longer on top and silky to the touch.

Ally heard a sound, a gruff, low sound that dragged at her nipples and lower, at her pelvis. It took a moment to realise it was Angelo, the sound a rough growl from the back of his throat.

Delight shimmered through her and a new sense of purpose and power. For the first time since she'd woken on this island Ally felt strong, almost invincible. The sound of his desire did that to her. The proof of his hunger.

As if kissing Angelo, and discovering he shared the same need, made her feel whole. More than whole. Right.

It was the most extraordinary, unexpected feeling. And she couldn't get enough of it.

Ally murmured encouragement against his lips as she threaded her fingers through his hair, shuffling still closer, discovering a ridge of potent hardness against her belly and—

Strong fingers settled on her upper arms and pushed her away. It took a moment to realise what was happening as she clung, limpet-like and lost in wonder.

Finally she blinked open heavy eyelids, her

breathing ragged and her body feeling as if she'd run a mile. And wanted to run more.

Angelo's eyes were so dark she couldn't distinguish iris from pupil. He stared back intently, his hair rumpled and sexy, his lips parted and skin pulled tight over those amazing bones.

He looked like a fallen angel, dark, sensuous and utterly beguiling. Some hitherto dormant part of her brain came abruptly to life and she realised that was what his name meant. *Angel.* But definitely a fallen angel.

Ally sighed. If he weren't holding her from him she'd have lifted her hands to the back of his skull and pulled his head back to hers.

As it was, it took long, long moments of gasping breaths to come down from the sensual high where he'd taken her.

Tiny shudders ran under her skin, down her thighs and between them, across her nipples and up her backbone. Every part of her quivered with what she could only assume was unsated sexual hunger.

Her gaze dropped to his mouth, his lips darker than before and parted as he too dragged in great gulps of air.

That was a relief. At least she wasn't alone in feeling this way.

'Is it always like this?' Ally didn't have time to censor the words. She needed to understand.

'Sorry?' Sleek dark eyebrows scrunched as if he couldn't make sense of a simple question.

'Between us. Is it always like this?'

Emotions flickered across his taut features. So quickly she couldn't pin them down. Finally he shook his head. 'It was just a kiss.'

Just a kiss?

She felt as if he'd turned her inside out. Or, more accurately, as if together they'd soared close to the sun.

His gaze shifted from hers and Ally realised he was lying. Or at least avoiding a direct answer.

'What are you scared of, Angelo?'

That dragged his attention back to her. 'Scared? Me?'

He made a scoffing noise but it wasn't nearly as convincing as that deep-throated groan of pleasure that even now swirled in the back of her mind. It had been the most glorious sound.

'Yes, you. If it was only a kiss why avoid answering? It's a simple enough question.'

For a second, gazes locked, Ally felt the connection they'd shared mere moments ago. Even his hands on her arms softened, his thumbs stroking through the plush material of her robe as she canted towards him, feeling the thick fabric graze her bare skin.

Then, abruptly, Angelo let her go and stepped back. A long pace that put an acre of distance between them.

His eyelids lowered as if to conceal the expression glittering there as he surveyed her.

It did no good. She *felt* the intensity of that stare.

If the connection between them had always been so strong, it must have taken something incredible to sever their marriage.

Slowly he shook his head. 'I should never have kissed you. It was a mistake. Especially since you seem to have read too much into a simple kiss—'

'No! Don't lie.' Ally folded her arms over her chest and tried to ignore the scratch of fabric across her nipples. 'It wasn't a simple kiss. You said it yourself before you kissed me. You said I couldn't have come here by accident because of this...' she waved her arm between them 'this... thing between us.'

'You can put that down to the emotional baggage we share. Our relationship is definitely over. Though by turning up here it seems you have trouble accepting that.'

'It doesn't feel over.' She jutted her chin and dared him to deny it.

'Okay.' He lifted one shoulder as if trying to dislodge a little stiffness. 'I admit I was curious after all this time. But it's not an experiment I want to repeat.'

No, because you got burned. Because the fire between us is anything but gone, no matter what you say.

'The past is the past,' he insisted, and Ally wondered if he was trying to persuade her or himself. 'There's nothing here for you any more. I'm not interested in you. I don't want you any more.'

Liar.

His unblinking stare and belligerent stance were a masquerade to hide the fact he *had* wanted her just moments ago. She couldn't have imagined that.

Anyone seeing him from a distance would be convinced by his show of disdain. Not Ally. She'd felt the need welling inside him. Heard it, experienced it at a primal level that left no room for doubt. She knew they shared something powerful. A longing he fought with all his considerable determination. Even now she felt the golden shimmer of anticipation in the air between them.

'Maybe you're right,' she said finally. If she wanted answers she had to play his game. 'But the emotions run hot and heavy between us.' She watched his eyes flare but he said nothing. 'Help me understand what's going on so I don't…misinterpret things again. Tell me what happened.'

Angelo looked into eyes the colour of lilac in spring and felt something shift within him. A momentary weakening, he assured himself. It had been a long, long time since he'd fallen for this woman's lies. He wouldn't do it again. He'd learned from his mistake.

So what was that kiss if not weakness?

And why was the compulsion not just to kiss her, but possess her totally, stronger than anything he could recall?

Surely he'd never felt like this about her before?

Alexa had been available and eager to please. She hadn't loved him nor he her. He wasn't even sure he was capable of that, because he'd never yet felt about a woman the way his parents had felt for each other.

He'd witnessed their love and assumed, one day, he'd feel the same about someone, until he'd seen his mother almost destroyed by her adored husband's death. Since then he'd been wary of romance. He couldn't bear to risk the shattering pain of losing his other half.

Losing his father had been grief enough, compounded by the need to fulfil his promise to care for his mother and sister as well as the family bank. That had stretched him so thin for so long he'd been almost glad to put barriers between himself and the women he dated. He'd had no emotional energy to spare for anything more than short-term affairs firmly anchored in sex with no other expectations.

Yet he remembered his mother's romantic tale about locking eyes on his father and knowing instantly that he was *the one*.

The one!

If his ex-wife was the one, it was the one major disaster in his life.

The one mistake he'd never forget.

The one woman he'd never trust again.

Which made his actions totally bizarre. He'd kissed her out of frustration and found himself falling into... He had no word for it. Angelo refused to countenance ideas like *bliss* or *desire*. Not with her.

Though he knew he'd spend a sleepless night trying to explain why kissing her now had felt new and different and compelling. As if there was something more than convenient sex between them.

'You want to know about the divorce?' His voice sounded strained and he realised he spoke through a clenched jaw.

'It would help.'

Angelo doubted it, but if it meant she kept her distance...

'Why don't you take a seat?'

After all, she was still recuperating.

'I'm fine. I'd rather you just told me.'

'We met in Rome, at a party.'

She nodded, eyes bright, hands clasped together as if eager for more.

Because she had no memories of the past? Or because she hoped to open up communication between them and wheedle her way back into his world? He wished he knew. Every time he thought he did, she made him doubt.

'We went back to my place that night.'

Her eyes rounded and she blinked. If Angelo didn't know better he'd even believe she blushed, but it had to be a trick of the light. His ex wasn't shy about sex. Far from it.

'And then?'

He shrugged. 'You stayed. I had business in Rome. A few days later, when I came here for a summer holiday, you came too.'

It had seemed simple. He'd been working even harder than usual and had looked forward to a short break. Alexa had been fun at first and easy company.

'And I stayed? As simple as that?' Her brow

furrowed as if wondering about commitments and work obligations. Five years ago none of that had mattered to her.

'Yes, you loved it here. The sea and relaxed lifestyle.'

She'd seemed genuinely happy. In retrospect Angelo was sure it hadn't been merely the chance to latch onto him as a meal ticket.

Alexa, no—she wanted to be Ally—frowned and looked towards the sea. 'I assume it's beautiful in good weather.'

'There's nowhere like it. Tourists come from the other side of the world to visit the Amalfi Coast and Capri.'

Fortunately fewer made it out to this smaller island, but the climate, architecture, scenery and food were the best in the world as far as Angelo was concerned.

His father's family had come from here generations ago and some of his most precious memories, of when his father was still alive, centred around summers holidaying in the region. Those halcyon days were the reason he'd bought this estate when he wanted a private escape.

'Okay, I loved it here.' Her gaze met his then danced away and he heard an unspoken question. Had she loved him, or he her?

His mouth firmed. The sooner he disabused her of that fantasy, the better.

'There was no great romance, if that's what you're thinking, Ally.' He paused, tasting her new name on his tongue. Strange how easily it came. 'We weren't in love.'

'Okay.' She looked doubtful but nodded. 'So it was a casual fling?'

'Something like that. I wasn't looking for a life partner.'

At twenty-nine he'd had more than enough to cope with at the helm of the family bank. His father had left a gaping hole and it had taken everything Angelo had to take his place and face down the doubters who thought the Ricci kid couldn't handle the job. That, and the need to prop up his grieving family, meant Angelo had had precious little time for a personal life.

Now those doubters were eating their words, and happily raking in profits as the bank outperformed most financial institutions, despite recent seismic shifts in the sector.

Ally wrinkled her nose in a way he'd noticed once or twice. The effect was…cute. Not in keeping with the sophisticated image she used to project.

Because her injury had affected her and she

wasn't so good at maintaining that image? Or had she changed over the years? Curiosity stirred.

'Why did we marry if we weren't in love?'

She made it sound as if no one married for any other reason which, given their history, was laughable.

'Because you came to me with proof you were pregnant.'

It was like setting off a bomb. She goggled up at him, her face changing colour as she swayed on her feet.

Angelo almost reached out to steady her but she found her footing and straightened her shoulders. He watched her hand slide across her belly. Was that a conscious gesture, designed to convince him she couldn't remember?

This constant doubt messed with his head. He turned and paced away, swivelling round to find her not looking at him but into space. She looked bewildered. And bereft.

He marched back, hating the way her expression made him feel.

'No, you're not a mother and you didn't lose the child.' Belatedly he realised his words were too abrupt but instinct urged him to eliminate any doubt in her mind as soon as possible.

Slowly her head turned and her eyes sought his. 'It was a mistake, then? I wasn't pregnant?'

Angelo felt her confusion and shock and almost reached out to take her hands. She looked in need of support.

Hell! It was only a couple of days since she'd washed up on the beach. Guilt bit him. He wasn't managing this well.

'Come.'

He ushered her to the armchair and watched her subside abruptly, as if her knees gave way.

When she was settled he took the chair opposite.

'There was no baby.'

She opened her mouth to question him but Angelo raised his hand. Better if she just let him tell the story.

'You'd been here for six weeks. I'd had to return to the mainland to work after a couple of weeks but you stayed on. I commuted, staying here every weekend and working a couple of days a week from here. But in all that time you didn't leave.'

Her brows twitched as if she didn't understand the significance of that, but it was something Angelo had checked and double-checked, given what happened later. Nor had she had any visitors.

'Then one day you travelled to the mainland for an appointment. A medical appointment.'

He paused, taking in the way Ally leaned forward as if eager for more. Did she really not know?

'When I saw you that evening you were shocked but excited. Somehow, despite being on the pill, you'd got pregnant but you hadn't told me of your suspicions because you thought it couldn't happen. Then you showed me the foetal scan taken that day with your name on it, and a letter outlining your follow-up appointments with a gynaecologist.'

Angelo grimaced at the sour tang filling his mouth. 'Marriage wasn't on my radar but I love my family and I know my duty. I knew too that I'd love my child, no matter how it was conceived.'

A pang of regret pierced him. Would he ever know what it was to care for a child of his own? His lifestyle, reinforced by the lesson of distrust that he'd learned from this woman, made it less likely.

'We married out of *duty*?'

Her voice sounded small and wary and Angelo narrowed his eyes, trying to read her expression.

'What's wrong with that?' He frowned. 'I believed myself responsible for a new life coming into the world. I couldn't walk away from that.'

She surveyed him silently and Angelo had the feeling she was weighing him up. What did she see?

'Even if it meant marrying someone you didn't love?'

He hitched one shoulder. 'You think I should have chosen personal preference over fatherly responsibility?'

Ally sat back. 'Marriage isn't a necessity between parents these days. Or am I wrong?' Her brow twitched as if she grappled with the question. 'What you're talking about doesn't sound like a recipe for a happy marriage.'

Angelo snorted. 'You're right there.' But not for the reasons she implied. 'Yet, far from having doubts about marriage, you jumped at the idea.'

He should have seen that as a warning and taken his time. Instead he'd been young and firmly focused on his duty to his unborn child. He'd been inspired by his own father, determined to be the sort of father his own had been.

Though he and Alexa didn't love each other, he'd told himself they could work to create a nurturing family for their child. Having seen grief turn his mother into a shadow of herself, he'd even welcomed the fact that their marriage would be based on necessity rather than romantic attachment. He would love his child, that was enough.

He'd been conceited enough to believe he was in control of the situation, never doubting he was doing the right thing in offering marriage. Angelo shook off the thoughts. 'We married quickly and privately but it didn't last long. Within months I discovered it had been a lie. You weren't pregnant.'

'I *what*?'

He shrugged, the movement tugging at the rigid muscles of his shoulders and neck. 'There was no pregnancy. You'd faked it, and the so-called proof from the doctor.'

He, who'd thought himself awake to the ways of the world, had been sucked in by her lies. That had been a blow to his ego and more, he'd actually grieved the loss of a baby who'd never been real.

The news had shattered his self-belief. Already stressed by the challenge of proving himself professionally to a board and financial pundits waiting for him to fail, the realisation he'd been duped so completely, and about something so important, had made him question his judgement more than anything else could have.

Ally gaped at him, mouth working, and he

realised he'd had enough. He had to end this quickly.

'Your plan was to fake a miscarriage but you were found out. Rosetta suspected things weren't what they seemed. When I confronted you and you realised you couldn't get away with lying you admitted it. For a while you tried to pretend you'd lied because you were in love and desperate to be with me. But you weren't convincing.' He paused, watching his words sink in. 'You wanted me for the money. The lifestyle. The husband who'd support you in style so you never had to work again.'

'Maybe I *was* in love.' She scowled at him. 'Maybe you misjudged me and it was all a terrible mistake.'

Bitterness filled him. Angelo had experienced love with his family and knew what he'd shared with her was too shallow to deserve the name.

He looked into Ally's apparently earnest eyes and felt himself wishing things could have been different. That *they'd* been different. Not because she could ever be the sort of woman he could love, but because for so long he'd felt empty inside.

Maybe it was time to make changes in his life, forget casual affairs and search for something more satisfying. Because after all these years he finally admitted he wanted something more.

The truth that he'd avoided for years was that he'd run scared of meaningful relationships with a woman.

Angelo remembered his grief when his father had died and he'd witnessed grief almost destroy his mother. He'd shunned anything that might bring him such pain, like a relationship that might make him vulnerable because he cared too much. He'd stuck to shallow sexual relationships because it seemed safer.

The irony was that policy had led to his affair with Alexa. In a twist of fate, by holding himself back from the possibility of a real relationship, he'd fallen into the trap set by a woman who saw only his bank balance. She'd targeted him because he could give her a life of luxury and because of that the people he loved had suffered.

Because of *his* error of judgement.

'It wasn't a mistake.' His voice was gruff. 'It was a calculated lie.'

She frowned. 'Maybe I was trying to get your attention the only way I could. If I loved—'

'Enough!' He refused to let her bandy that word about. 'Don't try to rewrite history. You didn't love me. You admitted it when I challenged you. In fact you seemed pleased at the way you'd fooled me.'

He'd been left feeling that, far from experiencing unrequited love, Alexa's feelings towards him and men in general were much more negative.

Now he watched her stunning eyes grow wide. If this was an act, she was impressive.

'So we divorced. You've never set foot in one of my homes since the day I discovered the truth about you, and that's how I prefer it. We've had no contact since.'

CHAPTER SIX

ALLY STARED IN the bathroom mirror, trying to read something, anything, into the image she saw there.

But, like mirrors the world over, it gave no clue to her character. She saw an ordinary woman with hair that in today's bright sunlight looked dark blonde instead of light brown. Her mouth was pinched and there were shadows under her eyes but those spoke of tiredness and stress, not personality.

The only noteworthy thing about her was the colour of her eyes. The vivid blue-purple colour of jacaranda blossom.

Yet even that unusual shade didn't spark any insights.

You've never set foot in one of my homes since the day I discovered the truth about you, and that's how I prefer it.

Ally forced down bile at the memory of Angelo's words yesterday. They were engraved in her brain, especially after a night when she'd tossed and turned, fruitlessly trying to switch off her thoughts long enough to get some rest.

Just her luck that a brain that couldn't remember anything earlier than a few days ago should have perfect recall, not just of his words but Angelo's tone and expression as he'd said them.

As if he tasted something disgusting on his tongue.

As if he never wanted to be reminded of their shared past.

Ally couldn't blame him. She was disgusted too.

Her skin crawled when she thought of faking a pregnancy to get a man to marry her. Her mind kept shying away from what Angelo had said, that she'd done it for purely mercenary reasons. But even if that weren't the case, even if she'd acted out of love and the need to be with him, that didn't excuse her actions.

How could she have done that?

How could she have thought it a reasonable thing to do yet be so horrified by it now? Did that mean she'd changed? Or was her dismay due to the fact she'd been found out?

Surely not. Ally just couldn't imagine doing anything so devious or venal. But perhaps her mind was playing tricks and one day soon she'd get her memory back and discover he wasn't the only man she'd tried to dupe.

She wrapped her arms around herself, shivering.

No wonder Angelo didn't want her here.

Now the attitude of his housekeeper, Rosetta, made sense.

She'd been here through their relationship. She'd had doubts about the pregnancy and knew Ally had lied. It was a miracle the woman continued to check on her and bring her delicious food. Given her severe demeanour, Ally guessed she was firmly on the side of her employer and saw Ally as trouble.

An hour ago, when Ally had taken her breakfast tray downstairs, she'd seen Rosetta's stare turn piercing with suspicion. As if she thought Ally aimed to wheedle her way into her good graces.

It had taken all Ally's courage to go downstairs. Physically she felt stronger so the stairs weren't a problem, but facing anyone after what Angelo had revealed took more courage than she thought she had.

But Gran had always said that sooner or later you had to face the consequences of your actions and it was better to do it sooner.

Ally was turning towards the bedroom when her brain clicked into action.

She planted a palm on the bathroom counter and leaned in hard, her breath a sharp gasp.

Gran? She had a gran?

Slowly, not daring to hope, she pondered the word. Not Nanna or Grandma but Gran. A definite person.

Yet when she tried to delve deeper and put a face to the name she hit that infuriating blank wall. The misty nothingness that fuzzed her thoughts when she tried too hard to remember.

Frustration rose. She sensed that for the first time she was close to a genuine memory. Yet pushing only stressed her and left her feeling useless and scarily empty.

Looking down at her fingers splayed on the marble counter she told herself it was a positive step. It was something from her past.

She had a grandmother and, by the sound of it, one who was sensible and cared about her. That was a positive, right?

It beat being told she was a scheming liar hands down.

Excitement stirred. It was the first sign she'd had that her memories might be accessible. True, she couldn't recollect a specific event, but knowing she had a gran and remembering her words had to count for something.

Relief shuddered through her. For days she'd

feared the doctor was wrong and she might have to face the rest of her life with no memory of her past.

Her eyes squeezed shut as she thought of those fragments of her past she knew about. The bits Angelo had told her. Instantly her stress levels hiked up as tension filled her.

Was it weak, not to want to face this? The constant disapproval? The knowledge she wasn't wanted?

Surely she'd recover more quickly somewhere else. Ally turned to look out at the spectacular view of terraced gardens, cobalt sea and azure sky. The weather had finally cleared. Maybe it was time to find somewhere else to recover.

Angelo tried to focus on emails but his thoughts kept straying.

To last night's kiss. To the yearning that had opened up inside him for more than just the taste of her.

It was utterly, irrefutably wrong to lust after his ex-wife. It should be out of the question. Yet Angelo couldn't lie to himself. He'd been on the brink of taking things too far.

With a woman he couldn't trust.

A woman he'd told himself he hated.

Yet she'd got underneath his skin in ways that

defied logic and his determination to keep her at a distance.

Everything about that kiss had felt fresh and wonderful. There'd been no taint of past lies. Instead it had felt like a new beginning. What enticement had she woven around him?

He'd had yet another discussion with the doctor, who was adamant that his ex-wife's memory loss was the result of head trauma. Adamant too that she needed rest and calm.

That, combined with the guilt that clawed Angelo's belly whenever he thought of last night's revelations, left him ill at ease.

He could have handled it better. Yet whenever he dealt with Ally he found himself running on emotion, not logic. Beneath every contact were memories of her bare-faced lies and selfish greed.

She'd hurt not only Angelo but his family. *That* had been unforgivable.

He'd promised his papà he'd look after the family, yet it was *he* who'd introduced Alexa and her poison into their lives. Because of him *they'd* suffered. Angelo had failed them, breaking his deathbed promise to the man he'd admired above all others. That knowledge carved a gash through his soul.

His mamma had been thrilled at the prospect of a *bambino*. She'd come alive for the first time since Angelo's father died, finally focusing on the future not the past.

His heart had lightened and he'd found himself for the first time thinking about a family of his own.

Then when the truth emerged he'd had to watch his beloved mamma withdraw into herself all over again.

And his sister grow wary to the point of paranoia. Giulia was a lovely person with her own unique beauty, yet she feared falling into the same trap as Angelo. She rarely dated, suspecting men were only attracted by her fortune, and he feared she was in danger of becoming a recluse. His once bright, gregarious sister!

That was Angelo's fault. If he hadn't fallen for Alexa's lies, acting impetuously with a youth's confidence in his own judgement, they wouldn't have suffered.

Yet that hadn't prevented his response to Ally. Despite the negative memories and suspicion, there was an insistent tug that kept drawing him to her. Physical attraction, yes, but something more too.

He was torn between wanting to protect her and make her smile and wishing she'd leave and never return.

Angelo raked his hand through his hair, swearing under his breath, and looked up to see he wasn't alone. Ally stood in the doorway, her hand raised as if to knock.

Like last night she wore that voluminous towelling robe and like last night he had no trouble imagining her naked body beneath it.

Angelo snagged a rough breath and surged to his feet.

The sooner she had new clothes so he wasn't constantly seeing her half-dressed, the better. He glanced at his watch. With the fine weather, Rosetta had left for the mainland and its shops early. Any time now—

'I won't keep you long. I'm sure you're busy.'

Ally's voice was crisp. He wished he felt half so businesslike around her. Instead he felt too much. It was a new and disturbing sensation.

'Come in.'

He gestured for her to take a seat before his desk.

'I prefer to stand.'

Jaw set, hands clasped before her and shining hair loose around her shoulders, she looked like a teenager called before the headmaster. Until he looked into her eyes and read determination.

'What can I do for—'

'I'd like to leave.'

'Leave?'

Angelo scowled. It was the last thing he'd expected. Surely her reason for being in the area was to get back into his home? Even if she had amnesia it was the only logical explanation.

'Yes, please.' Her gaze flickered and he realised she wasn't as sure of herself as she tried to project. 'Now the weather's improved I can get to the mainland, can't I?'

Surprise shot through him. 'You have somewhere in mind?'

Was she finally going to admit to her scheme?

She shook her head, her mouth thinning. 'No. But I thought, in the circumstances...' She waved her hand vaguely around his study. 'You don't want me here and I can understand, given what you told me.' Her voice wobbled a little and she swallowed. 'I'd like to think I had a reason for what I did. That my motives weren't as simple as you believe. But I just don't *know*. All I know is I hate what you've told me and it makes me uncomfortable being here.'

Heat drilled from Angelo's gullet to his belly.

Shame. A searing streak of fire that made him shift his weight. He had every right not to trust her and everything he'd told her was true, but that didn't alter the fact she was injured and needed care. Where was his decency? So much for living up to his *papà*'s example.

The doctor's words rang in his head.

Care, rest and quiet. That's what she needs. No stress.

Yet she was asking to leave because she felt uncomfortable here.

So she should, after the way she'd behaved.

Yet Angelo had to rise above that. He knew his duty to a guest, much less an injured one. Besides, if he wanted to learn the reason for her presence, he needed to keep an eye on her.

'I'm sorry you're uncomfortable. But I don't think you realise the damage done by that storm,' he said eventually. 'Many coastal towns were hit. Hospitals are full and emergency services are stretched. If anyone on the mainland has room to spare they're hosting neighbours whose homes have been wrecked.'

'I see.' She swung her head to look out at the garden, her nose wrinkling in that trademark move he'd come to realise meant she was thinking hard.

'Look, Ally.' It got easier all the time to use her new name. Maybe because memories of Alexa were so poisonous. The name Ally didn't have the same negative connotations. 'You're welcome to stay here.'

'Welcome?' Her eyebrows disappeared under her fringe.

'Yes.' He held her eyes, ignoring the throb of energy that passed between them and focusing on what had to be done. 'There's plenty of room here and, whatever our past, you're *safe*. And it would be better if the same doctor could monitor you, don't you think?'

He paused to let that sink in. 'I admit I reacted badly when you arrived.' With sound reason. 'But the past is the past. Maybe you've done me a favour. It's done me good to confront that finally.'

He still couldn't relax around her but he realised, with a flash of insight, hoarding hatred all these years wasn't healthy. He'd thought of how his mother and sister had been scarred by his marriage breakup. He had been too, becoming suspicious and judgemental. Maybe it was time to cultivate the more generous side of his nature.

'You're injured and need help. I can provide that. Then when you're better you can move on.'

She stared as if she'd never seen him before and Angelo silently acknowledged that it was a significant turnaround, from enemy to ally. But he had an obligation to care for her till she was well enough to return to her normal life. Lashing out over her past actions did no one any good. She needed quiet to recuperate, not his jibes.

'And what—' she paused '—if I don't get my memory back?'

Her chin tilted high and she stood taller, as if shoring up her defences against such a possibility. Angelo glimpsed fear in her eyes and felt the hard kernel of bitterness inside him melt a little. She was trying to be strong though she clearly feared the worst.

Angelo moved from behind the desk and walked towards her, stopping at arm's length. 'According to the doctor that's extremely unlikely. He thinks that the best prescription for regaining your memory is rest and a lack of stress, both of which you can get here.' He breathed deep. 'I promise to be a better host and—'

'There's no need. I understand why you don't like having me around.'

That wasn't quite true. Mainly he'd prefer she'd never come. Yet part of him was fascinated and wanted to discover what it was about her that drew him so relentlessly.

'I haven't behaved well,' he admitted, 'and that pains me.' He was a proud man but he'd been raised to be decent, not a bully. 'Let me make it up to you. How about a truce? I'll try to set the past aside and you try not to worry about the future and we'll see how we go.'

Suspicion glinted in her narrowed eyes. 'Why would you do that?'

'Because I don't like the man I become when I dwell on the past.'

The words surprised him. He'd only just acknowledged that their shared past had changed him. And realised he wanted to move in a more positive direction. He hadn't meant to blurt it out. But it seemed to have been the right thing to say because she nodded and her high shoulders sank a fraction.

'I don't like the woman I was in the past either.'

Angelo scoured her features, wondering how much he could trust her words. Were they designed to lure him into trusting her?

It would drive him insane if he second-guessed her every move. He had to stop that. What could she do to him anyway? Forewarned was forearmed so there was no possibility she'd dupe him again.

'Then how about we focus on the present?'

Still she hesitated. 'And if my memory doesn't return?'

'We'll take the doctor's advice. In a week or so, if there's no change, no doubt he'll organise more tests.'

Angelo watched Ally consider that. Strange that, when she finally nodded assent, he felt relief.

'You've got a deal.' She stepped forward, extending her hand, something Angelo didn't remember from the past. She'd preferred kisses on the cheek.

'Deal.' His hand met hers and he was surprised by her firm, businesslike handshake.

Ally shook his hand, feeling for a change as if she weren't totally powerless. 'Excellent. I'll do my best not to get under your feet.'

The words were calm but clipped and she felt proud of herself, given the way her emotions had wobbled all over the place.

She slipped her hand from his. Maybe her job made her a confident speaker, or at least able to appear confident. Was she a teacher? Lawyer? Journalist? Certainly she'd felt at home shaking hands, even if the tingle along her palm and fingers proved this man still had the power to rouse her.

But there'd be no more kisses. No more getting carried away. No matter how much she craved the mindless physical pleasure of it. Craved this man.

It was as if she had a long-standing addiction to him that even time, disgrace, shame and willpower couldn't conquer.

Ice trickled down her backbone as she remembered what he'd told her. That she'd trapped him for his money. It must be true. His housekeeper would back him up on that, yet Ally couldn't get her head around the idea.

Far better to do what he suggested and concentrate on the present.

'One thing before we move on.'

Angelo's deep voice burred through her, making her wonder what it would be like if he didn't want to move on. If instead he wanted to devote his attention to a woman, not because he distrusted her but because he desired her.

Ally's pulse raced, that flicker of heat stirring again, despite her attempts to stop it.

'Yes?'

The single syllable was husky as her throat constricted. She hated that she was drawn to him sexually. It felt like a betrayal by her body yet she didn't know how to stop it.

'I'm sorry for distressing you when I told you about the past. I could have found a better way to tell you.'

Ally stared up into unfathomable dark eyes. No, not quite unfathomable. In the past she'd read anger and distaste there. Then passion. Now she saw regret.

It made him look human. Appealing. Too attractive.

That was all she needed…

'Reliving our past brought a lot of long-buried feelings to the surface. It won't happen again.'

'Thank you, Angelo.' The apology felt significant. An acknowledgement that she wasn't the only one who'd behaved badly.

Carefully she surveyed him and once more glimpsed a different man. One who wasn't hard or brooding.

What had he been like when they'd first met? Surely not so dour. Had he been charming? Seductive?

Had she fallen in love with him five years ago?

She blinked as the suspicion took hold. Could that really be why she'd behaved so appallingly?

It might explain why she was attracted to him now, when everything she knew about their past made her cringe with shame. Was it some subconscious recollection of her deeper feelings for him?

Ally's breath seized. She only remembered to breathe when she caught movement in her peripheral vision and noticed Rosetta in the doorway. The housekeeper's expression was blank but her eyes burned. With suspicion?

Hurriedly Ally stepped away from Angelo as the other woman said something in Italian.

'Excellent,' Angelo said. 'Bring them in.'

Her face set, Rosetta moved closer and Ally realised the woman understood English. Communication between them had been limited, the other woman choosing not to speak, and Ally had assumed it was because of a language barrier.

Heat flushed her cheeks as she realised Rosetta had simply preferred not to talk to her. Because of what had happened before. The skin across Ally's shoulders and nape crept tighter as if skeletal fingers pinched her there.

Had she really been so appalling?

She let out a shuddering breath. The answer to that was clear.

The woman held out two big shopping bags to her.

'Rosetta went to the mainland to get you some clothes.'

'You did?'

She needed clothes, badly. All she had was a T-shirt and bikini. And the use of this robe and some shirts for sleeping that must be Angelo's. She'd recovered enough to find that disturbing. Though they smelled of sunshine and fresh soap rather than potent male, she couldn't help being aware of whose they were as the cotton brushed her skin.

'Thank you so much, Rosetta. That was good of you. I appreciate it.'

She guessed the other woman had a busy schedule given the pristine state of the mansion and the exquisite food she prepared.

'You're welcome.' Ally caught her surprise, quickly masked. 'You needed something decent and my clothes wouldn't fit you.'

At the word *decent* Ally felt her blush intensify, conscious of the robe that gaped a little as she bent to accept the bags. Rosetta barely came up to her shoulder. No wonder Ally had been given Angelo's shirts in lieu of pyjamas instead of borrowing something from her.

'Aren't you going to look at them, to see if they fit?' Angelo asked. 'Rosetta took your swimsuit as a size guide but still...'

'Of course.'

Yet she felt self-conscious as she put the bags on a chair and plunged her hand into one. She withdrew it to discover she'd grabbed a handful of black lace, a see-through bra and G-string, not the T-shirt and shorts she'd expected.

Hurriedly she shoved them back down, feeling the tips of her ears burn. She was *not* holding those up against herself.

Interesting, though, that Rosetta had chosen that underwear. What had Ally expected? Cotton? Something plain and practical? If so, what did that tell her?

Putting the idea aside, she delved into the second bag and withdrew a strappy sundress in a delicate floral print of pinks and lavender blue.

'Oh!' She held the fabric against her. 'How pretty. Thank you, Rosetta.' The material was a soft cotton that draped beautifully. 'I love it.'

She looked across to find two sets of eyes fixed on her, both looking startled.

What had she said? Ignoring the puzzle, Ally smiled at the housekeeper. 'I'm sure it will be a good fit and if it needs adjustment maybe I could borrow a needle and thread?'

Rosetta nodded slowly. 'Of course.'

Still the other woman looked at her strangely. Ally told herself to ignore it, delving further into the bag to discover more clothes, this time in solid colours, cut stylishly. They looked trendy and well-made but maybe a bit dressy for around the house.

'Thank you,' she said again, looking from Rosetta to Angelo. 'Can you give me the receipt please, so I know how much I owe you?'

Ally heard a choking noise that could have been shock or disparagement, then the housekeeper said something in Italian and, at a nod from Angelo, left the room.

'What did I say? Is something wrong?' The

housekeeper already disapproved of her and Ally
didn't want to get her further offside.

'Nothing's wrong.'

Yet his tone and quizzical look said otherwise.

Ally put the clothes down. 'Please, Angelo.
We called a truce, didn't we? I'd rather you told
me what the problem is.' Surely nothing he said
would be as upsetting as the facts he'd already
shared.

He spread his hands in a gesture that struck her
as intrinsically Italian. 'No problem. Just something interesting.'

'Go on.'

He tilted his head to one side as if taking stock
of some curiosity. 'First, you looked uncomfortable with the lingerie Rosetta chose. But in the
past you had no qualms about wandering around
the house in just that.'

Ally blinked, trying and failing to picture herself letting anyone else see her in those tiny wisps
of nothing.

'Second, the one item you gushed about didn't
have a designer label.'

Ally folded her arms. 'Let me guess. In the past
I only wore expensive clothes?'

Angelo shrugged. 'They were your preference
and I know for a fact you never wear florals. Your
taste in clothes is more…dramatic.'

Ally's forehead twitched as she looked again at the clothes. Of the lot, the one that appealed most was the sundress. It seemed her tastes had changed in half a decade.

'Anything else? No, let me guess.' She swallowed, hating what she knew was coming. 'That I intend to pay you for the clothes.'

Slowly he nodded. 'That and the fact you mentioned altering it to fit. Your strengths didn't lie in dressmaking.'

Heat swirled deep inside as Ally thought of what she *had* been good at. Lying and sex, as far as she could tell. She lifted her chin. 'That was years ago. Obviously I've changed.'

For a second Angelo said nothing. Then he inclined his head and it felt like a win, as if the truce they'd called were real. 'Clearly you have.'

He gestured to something else Rosetta had brought. A small backpack embroidered with daisies. 'There's this too. The belongings you left in the locker on the mainland.'

Instantly Ally forgot about clothes and personality changes and reached for the pack. It was light, too light, if it held all her worldly possessions.

She clutched it close, trying and failing to be optimistic that this might jog her memory.

'Ally?' Was that concern on Angelo's face? It felt like it when he steered her to a deeply padded chair and guided her into it. 'It will be all right. I promise.'

His words, soft and deep, wrapped around her chest, easing the tight breath caught in her lungs. Making her realise she was, quite suddenly, terrified.

'Do you want me to open it?' The unexpected tenderness in his tone almost undid her. She could stand up for herself against aggression or disapproval. But against kindness...

'No. Thanks. It's fine.'

With trembling fingers she opened the fastening and upended the contents. Faded jeans. Sneakers, a blue T-shirt that said *Roma*, which she knew to mean Rome, a nude bra and knickers. A comb, lip balm, water bottle, sun cream and euros. She didn't know the currency so couldn't tell if it was a lot or a little.

Nothing to divulge her identity. No name tag or address. Worse, nothing familiar. Her hands strayed over the collection again and again, willing herself to remember, but nothing came. Just that yawning blank.

She shivered, the lip balm rolling off her lap.

'There's nothing,' she gasped. 'Nothing I can recall.'

Suddenly Angelo was there, squatting before her, holding her unsteady hands in his big, firm ones.

'It's early days. You need time. Ally, do you hear me?' His hands squeezed hers and she looked up to find his dark eyes glowing with concern.

A weight shifted inside her and she breathed again.

'Of course.' She wasn't sure she believed it but if she said it often enough… 'Soon I'll remember everything. Then I can go home.'

Ally's breath caught. *Home*. It sounded wonderful.

She just prayed she *would* remember where that was. And that she'd survive living with Angelo Ricci until then.

CHAPTER SEVEN

ALLY SMILED AS Enzo laughed. It was the happiest sound she'd heard in the four days she'd been here.

Her smile became a grin as she jammed the hat down, turning her head to give him a profile view as if she modelled haute couture instead of a tatty straw sunhat.

It was kind of him to produce the hat for the sun beat down brightly. The sky and sea were a brilliant blue and even the storm-battered garden was vivid with colour.

'The hat may be worn but it'll do the job. Thank you, Enzo. *Grazie.*'

It was one of her two bits of Italian, the other being *per favore*, which meant please.

He nodded and said something she didn't understand. It didn't matter. She'd puttered happily beside him in the garden for half an hour and gestures had been sufficient.

Ally kept catching her breath at the nooks and stunning vistas in this garden perched high above the sea. It was like something from a travel brochure or a sophisticated magazine. Stunningly beautiful.

Yet it wasn't familiar. Surely, as Angelo's ex-wife, she should feel *déjà vu*?

In Angelo's arms she'd experienced, if not *déjà vu*, then at least a sense of rightness, as if, finally, everything had fallen into place. Yet since then, nothing.

Shouldn't she remember the elegant wisteria loggia, where she'd found Enzo raking up leaves stripped by the storm? Or the rose arbour, sleepy with the hum of bees? Or the secluded pond with its exquisite marble statue of a boy fishing?

Each garden within a garden made her pause as pleasure washed through her.

That, she suspected, was why Enzo let her tag along. He saw how she admired the place. To her delight she even knew the names of some of the plants.

Did that mean she had a garden of her own somewhere? The idea tantalised but led nowhere. Her past was still a blank. Frustratingly, scarily so.

Putting on the gloves he'd provided, Ally gathered up bougainvillea cuttings and put them in the wheelbarrow. The hot pink cascade of battered flowers was so bright it almost hurt the eye and she paused, mesmerised.

Everything here seemed saturated with brightness and warmth, from the vibrant red geraniums to the blazing white of the garden balustrades against the opalescent sea beyond. It was so different to what she was used to. So—

'Ally? What are you doing?'

She blinked and shivered, vainly trying to grasp the thought that had entered her brain so easily and now disintegrated like a tantalising wisp of smoke.

Not what she was used to. Different to...what?

'Ally?' That deep voice was closer and the thought was gone. Completely disappeared.

She drew a shuddery breath and tried not to mind. Surely it would return. But dismay and frustration feathered her spine. Would she *ever* remember?

Warmth encompassed her bare elbow and she turned, gaze locking with eyes the colour of her morning espresso, rich, dark and addictive.

She blinked, scurrying to revise that thought. Not addictive. She wouldn't let it be so.

Even if she found herself thinking about Angelo too often. Even if her dreams featured a dark, enigmatic man who seduced her again and again, leaving her breathless and unsettled, wishing she weren't alone in her vast bed.

Wishing he'd take her in his arms and kiss her again.

No, no, no! She refused to go there.

'Hello, Angelo.'

Her voice was a husky croak that she feared betrayed her libidinous thoughts.

Because Angelo Ricci was extraordinarily handsome and he'd actually been pleasant these last couple of days. He'd been gentle and supportive when he'd presented the daypack with her meagre belongings and her hopes had taken a nosedive because they didn't spark recognition.

He'd been kind as well, giving her free run of the English language books in his library and organising new clothes for her. Not just any clothes. They were beautifully made and expensive. Rosetta had obviously been told to buy the best.

But Ally refused to find him addictive. Or attractive. Others might, but her taste ran to…

Her breath snagged. She had no idea what her taste in men was like.

Like Angelo Ricci, insisted the voice in her head.

Once she'd found pleasure with this man. Earthy sexual pleasure. For all his air of buttoned-down control, there was a raw masculinity about him, an air of sensuality, that beckoned to some breathless, needy part of her.

Ally stifled the thought.

'I thought you were going to read by the pool.'

He frowned down at her. Not with anger like before but with something that made her pulse trip faster because it made her feel cared for. How crazy was that? Was she so desperate for affection?

'I'm helping Enzo.' She ignored the catch to her voice, just as she ignored the way Angelo's hand on her elbow sent warmth spilling through her.

'You're supposed to be resting.'

There it was again. That note of concern appealed too much. She pulled free, not liking the way her nerve-endings sparked and crackled at the contact as if from an electric shock.

'I've been resting for days, Angelo. I got bored sitting by the pool. Besides, this is restful. I'm just strolling, passing tools to Enzo and putting a few prunings in the wheelbarrow. It's lovely to be in the garden.'

She didn't add that she'd also been drawn by the company. Rosetta had still to crack a smile in Ally's presence, though she wasn't quite so frowningly remote. And Angelo, despite his changed attitude, wasn't a comfortable presence. The undercurrent of awareness or doubt or whatever it was between them was palpable.

Ally fought it by peppering him with questions

at mealtimes. About Italy, his home, the island—anything impersonal. Because when things became personal between them everything got out of control.

Her blood effervesced whenever his hand brushed hers or she discovered him watching her, eyes glinting with something she couldn't identify.

Once or twice she'd imagined it was approval she saw there, even attraction. After all, he'd kissed her passionately. But then his expression would change and she knew she was fooling herself. Angelo had admitted to curiosity about kissing her. But now he'd moved on.

'You have to be careful not to overdo it.' He turned and spoke to Enzo in Italian.

Ally watched, frustrated. She'd felt at home pottering among the plants, like it was something she was used to doing. That, of itself, made her want to stick at it, in case it sparked a memory. It gave her hope, made her feel she was doing something useful.

It also kept her mind off her fraught relationship with her host.

'No, please.' Ally interrupted. 'Don't say I can't help.' She heard the desperation in her voice and stopped. After a breath she continued. 'Enzo's been very kind and I enjoy his company. I'm not doing any damage, I promise.'

Angelo stared down at her, wishing the brim of that disreputable hat didn't shadow her face.

Had he imagined that taut, woebegone look? The edge of panic in her tone?

That made him wonder if she should be in hospital after all. It would be easy to get her there now. But the doctor thought it best Ally stay quietly here. Which made her Angelo's responsibility.

'I'm sure the garden is in no danger from you.'

He smiled reassuringly, conscious as always of the disparity in their sizes. For despite her feistiness he'd been shocked to read something like fear in her eyes a couple of days ago. That look had stopped him in his tracks, making him abruptly aware that he loomed over her.

He'd felt shame course through him, an emotion he wasn't accustomed to, since he'd spent his life trying to be as honourable and honest as his father.

The woman he'd married had never looked at him with fear. She'd understood that, no matter how she provoked him, he was protective of women. He'd never resort to violence.

These past days had convinced Angelo that her

amnesia was real. Either that or she'd become the best actress he'd ever met.

As a result, his suspicions had taken a back seat. It was pointless reminding himself she'd used and betrayed him. That woman was a far cry from the one before him.

He liked this new Ally who asked so many questions about his homeland and its customs. Who seemed intrigued by everything and eager to discover more.

The Alexa he'd known had been more interested in his income than local traditions. Was it time that had changed her or simply memory loss?

And why that panic in her voice now? What was so wonderful about traipsing after Enzo? In the past she'd never seemed to notice anyone else when Angelo was around, especially staff.

'You can help Enzo later. It's time for his lunch break.'

'Oh, of course,' she said immediately, taking off her hat and gloves and putting them on the laden wheelbarrow. 'I hadn't realised the time. I didn't mean to keep him from his break.'

She approached Enzo, thanking him in halting Italian and winning an approving grin.

Angelo watched, intrigued. Enzo was Rosetta's

husband and knew the circumstances of Angelo's failed marriage. Yet the older man's response was warm.

She always was good at wrapping people around her little finger.

Angelo stifled the doubting voice as they walked towards the house. Ally wasn't bluffing about the amnesia. She'd been an accomplished liar in the past but over this she was telling the truth. Whatever her reason for returning, and knowing her she had a reason, he pitied her predicament. Shame stabbed him, as he remembered the harsh way he'd treated her. He'd tried to make that up to her, offering the care an injured guest deserved, and she seemed to be improving, physically at least.

Yet he was intrigued about the bond between her and his gardener.

Everything about her fascinated him. She seemed at the same time so familiar and yet so changed.

'You and Enzo get on well, considering he doesn't speak English.'

She shrugged. 'I suppose we have gardens in common. There's nothing quite like being out amongst growing things, is there?'

Angelo met a sideways glance from guileless eyes and felt as if he'd walked into a wall.

It was the sort of comment he expected from his mother, who loved tending her roses and herbs. Not his ex.

Had she undergone a personality transplant?

His wife had been lively, sociable and good at getting on with people. But always, he'd learned, for a purpose. Never had she expressed an interest in anything as domesticated as gardening. As for sewing or altering clothes, Angelo wouldn't have believed it except he'd heard it with his own ears.

This new Ally was a puzzle.

One he intended to solve.

More and more she disconcerted him. Even something as simple as walking beside her felt different. He was aware of the feminine contours of her body. Lusher and more pronounced than in the past. Maybe she wasn't dieting so strictly these days? Had she given up modelling?

Nor did she seem as tall. That had unnerved him till he realised it had to be because she wore flat shoes or went barefoot, whereas in the past she'd worn heels, even lazing around the poolside.

Small things but unsettling.

For the first time in years, five years to be precise, Angelo felt he wasn't in complete control of the situation. It wasn't a sensation he liked.

'So, you enjoy gardening,' he said as they took their seats on the terrace looking over the sea.

A wide awning gave shade and, like yesterday, Ally took her time admiring the view and the urns perched on the balustrade that overflowed with bright flowers.

'Apparently. I found it relaxing this morning. Besides, how could you not enjoy it with surroundings like these?'

Angelo always found it restful here, but seeing her admiration made him view it with new eyes.

Maybe he should listen to his family, who urged him to take more time off to enjoy the luxuries he'd worked so hard for, like this estate on an exclusive, sought after island. Perhaps there were changes he needed to make in his life.

'Is this your permanent home?'

'Sadly no. I spend more time in Rome and elsewhere.'

Ally frowned. 'But you spend a lot of time here, surely?'

She might have read his mind. Angelo shrugged, stifling discomfort. Because she was right, the place was special but he rarely allowed himself the downtime to enjoy it as he should. 'Not as much as I'd like.'

Her head tilted to one side. 'Why?' Then her eyes

rounded. 'It's not because of me, is it? Because coming here reminds you of what happened—?'

'No!' She looked so aghast he had to cut her off. 'Nothing like that. It's still a retreat for me, the place I come to get away.'

Strange that, though this was where he'd been with Alexa, it wasn't here that the painful past usually haunted him. It was when he was with his mother and sister, seeing the damage his fiasco of a marriage had inflicted on them.

The fact that the villa didn't usually evoke memories of Alexa showed how little she'd meant to him as a person. They'd never connected emotionally and there'd been no depth to their relationship. Just physical attraction then a sense of duty when she'd announced her pregnancy.

In fact, Angelo realised abruptly, he cared far more for her now than he had when they'd been lovers. He surveyed her sun-kissed features and rumpled hair and felt none of the anger he'd harboured so long.

'So why not visit more often?' When he didn't immediately respond she said, 'Not that it's any of my business.'

'It's a fair enough question.' He stared into those bright eyes and wondered why he didn't mind talking about it with her.

Because she was like a stranger? They said it was easier to talk about personal things with people who didn't know you.

He shrugged. 'Ever since I took over from my father I've devoted myself to business. I rarely take time off.'

When he did his time was punctuated with video conferences, calls and emails. Even his weekends here were interrupted by work.

'Ever since?' A tiny frown creased Ally's brow. 'Was there a problem when you took over?'

'It wasn't easy to begin with. My father died suddenly and—'

'I'm sorry. That must have been tough.'

Sympathy glowed in her eyes and to Angelo's amazement he felt his throat tighten. It was a long time since his *papà*'s death, yet he still missed him. Nor was he used to sympathy. He was the one who'd held everything together for his family. The one they looked to for support.

'Thank you. He was a special man.' He paused. 'I've worked hard to live up to his standards and, yes, there were lots of people who doubted I could fill his shoes. I was seen as inexperienced. But I've proved them wrong. The bank is an even bigger, more successful enterprise now.'

'I'm sure he'd be proud of you.'

Again she surprised him. Her empathy and insight were unexpected. Five years *had* changed her.

'I hope so.' Some thought ego had prompted him to try to outdo his father. Instead he'd worked to live up to his father's memory and provide for his mother and sister.

Later, after his divorce, his drive had been fuelled by the need to harness negative emotions and direct his energy somewhere positive. The failed marriage had dented his ego and confidence in his judgement, inflicting a burden of shame at not protecting his family, at letting his father down.

He'd been determined not to fall for any woman's wiles and had reinforced his policy of confining himself to brief hook-ups that were sexually satisfying and didn't interfere with his well-ordered world.

Strange that having his ex here made him wonder what a permanent relationship would be like. To make this place a home rather than a part-time retreat.

To be here with his wife and children.

He hadn't thought in those terms because thinking about starting a family was like probing an unhealed wound. Instinctively he'd retreated from the idea of making himself vulnerable to love, having seen loss devastate his mother. Then the debacle with Alexa had shut down a part of him. Was he a lesser man for that?

'But if the business is so successful, surely you can delegate and take more time off?'

Angelo focused on the woman across the table from him. 'You sound like my mother. She tells me to relax more and my sister...' He paused, realising that oddly he didn't mind mentioning them to Ally.

'Your sister?' she prompted.

'She calls me a workaholic.'

Ally released a gentle huff of laughter that whispered across his skin before curling deep inside, where he felt a nugget of glowing heat. 'I like the sound of your sister. Clearly she's a very brave woman.'

The glint in her eyes was teasing and Angelo's mouth crimped up at the corners. Giulia was the only other person who teased him. Strange that he enjoyed it now with Ally.

Maybe his family was right. Maybe it was time to reconsider what he wanted from life. Angelo had no plans to follow his father into an early grave. The divorce had changed him, made him bitter. Perhaps it was time to focus more on the positives.

'If I owned this place I wouldn't want to move.'

Ally waved a hand towards the view. 'Just look at that hot pink pelargonium trailing over the white of the balustrade with the deep blue sea beyond. It's stunning.'

Angelo sat back, watching Ally's enthralled expression and listening to her unvarnished enthusiasm.

When she'd been here before she'd loved the place but had been too sophisticated to gush about it. Now he found her appreciation engaging.

His thoughts were interrupted by Rosetta, arriving with bread and antipasti.

Ally enthused about the garden as they served themselves from the delectable spread. She seemed to know what she was talking about. She mentioned plants by name and was particularly interested in the garden's design and its different sections, or rooms as she called them.

'The rose arbour in particular...'

She trailed off as if lost in admiration at the memory.

Angelo nodded and reached for a bottle of sparkling water, topping up their glasses.

His mother was fond of that sheltered corner of the garden, with its rich scent and abundance of blooms. It struck him that she'd enjoy sharing this meal with Ally, discussing plants and design.

It was only as he put the bottle down that he realised Ally was sitting bolt upright and her expression was stunned. He leaned closer, concern rising, particularly at the way she held a piece of bread in the air as if frozen in the act of taking a bite.

'Ally?' His nape prickled. 'What is it?'

She didn't even blink.

'Ally!'

Still she seemed absorbed in something she could see beyond him. He swung round and noted a yacht in the distance but nothing else. Nothing to stun her into silence.

He shoved his chair back, worry rising, when she spoke.

'Gran,' she whispered, with such yearning in her voice that it stopped Angelo mid-movement.

He scoured her face for signs of pain or distress. All he found was a curious blankness that contrasted with a furrowed brow that spoke of concentration.

Then, abruptly, she sat back, blinking, her suspended hand dropping to the table, her eyes over-bright.

Angelo didn't stop to think. In a second he was around the table, crouching beside her chair. He covered her hand with his. Was it imagination or was her flesh chilled?

'Talk to me, Ally.'

Finally she swung her head around and he expelled a breath that felt like relief as her gaze caught his and he read recognition there. It had only lasted seconds but he'd felt unnerved by those moments when she'd been unresponsive, as if far away in her head.

Had she overdone it, helping Enzo? Had she somehow worsened the damage to her brain? Guilt stirred. He should have kept a better eye on her. Made her to rest.

'I remembered,' she whispered, so low that he had to lean close to hear. The scent of sweet neroli-scented soap and warm female flesh tickled his nostrils, distracting him for a second.

'You remembered? That's excellent.'

They'd been waiting for a sign that her memory would return. Angelo hadn't let himself think about what would happen if it never did. About the complications that would ensue if he had to play the host until they discovered enough for her to take up her life again.

Yet, instead of looking delighted, her face was drawn and her eyelashes spiked with tears.

He squeezed her hand. 'What did you remember, Ally? Your life? How you came here?'

She lifted her other hand to her face, wiping the

back of it across her eyes the way a child would brush tears from her face.

'Not that much. But it made me feel...' Her mouth wobbled and for a horrible moment it looked as if she'd cry.

Angelo had never seen this woman cry in all the time he'd known her. Even faced with recriminations when her lies were exposed, she'd been defiant rather than broken, certain rather than upset. The sight of her blinking back tears tugged at something deep inside him.

Angelo moved closer and wrapped his arms around her. Ally's head subsided against his shoulder, her hands clinging to his shirt as she sniffed.

'Sorry. I'm sorry,' she whispered.

She buried her face against his throat and he felt dampness on his skin. Despite all his caution Angelo also felt an upsurge of sympathy and protectiveness as he tightened his embrace. Whatever had happened, it had totally thrown her.

He held her firmly, feeling the tremors racking her body, the shaking breaths that heated his skin, the smudge of tears.

It felt different from any past embrace. He knew this woman and yet in this moment she felt unfamiliar.

No, that wasn't it. His body cradled hers easily, as if the weight of her slim frame against him was the most natural thing. It was her distress that was unusual. His ex-wife had never displayed fear or sadness, just an unwavering certainty that she had a right to whatever she wanted.

'Sorry, Angelo,' she said again. 'I don't know what came over me.'

She pulled back and, to his surprise, he was reluctant to release her.

Angelo tore his thoughts from that and focused on Ally. 'What happened? Did you remember something bad?'

She shook her head, sniffing, and smoothed her hair back from her face in a gesture he remembered from the old days.

Strange how the sight of her doing that, while wearing the pretty floral dress and blinking back tears, messed with his head. As if the unwelcome past melded with the present.

'No, nothing bad. That's what I don't understand. I should be happy to remember something, shouldn't I? And it was a nice memory.'

She blinked tear-glazed eyes and Angelo thought he'd never seen anything so sad yet so beautiful.

'Tell me about it.' He took her hand again, rubbing his thumb rhythmically over the back of it, ignoring the thud of his heart against his ribs.

For a second longer her eyes locked on his, as if frantic for reassurance. Then she looked away and Angelo felt it as an abrupt release of tension.

'It was the scent of the bread.' She lifted her other hand and he realised she still held a piece of focaccia.

'Rosetta is renowned for her baking.' Though in the past his ex hadn't indulged, too busy watching her intake of carbohydrates to eat even the best home-made bread.

'Not the bread. The rosemary sprinkled on top. That's what made me remember.'

She swallowed and it was easy to see she still battled strong emotion.

'Go on.'

She flashed him a lopsided smile that hit him hard. It wasn't practised or sultry but it was real, something Angelo found incredibly enticing.

He found *her* incredibly enticing. Not because she aroused protective instincts but because of her enthusiasm, her air of honesty, her lively interest in so many things.

Angelo waited for the cynical inner voice to crush that idea but for once it was silent. He didn't know whether to be relieved or concerned.

'I smelled the rosemary and it hit me. I remembered being on the veranda of a house, looking out over a garden. I was standing, pouring a rosemary hair rinse over a woman with white hair. My gran.' Her voice wobbled on the last word. 'I knew who she was even though I was behind her and couldn't see her face. We were talking about how well the rinse had turned out. One of my best yet.'

Angelo met Ally's bright eyes and read turbulent emotion there. Another new experience. In the past she'd revealed only what she wanted him to see. Now he sensed she wasn't even thinking about what she revealed. She was simply dealing with what her disordered mind had thrown up.

He frowned. 'Surely that's good? A positive memory about a person and a place? That's a start.'

She nodded, her lips crimping at the corners as if holding back emotion. 'You're right. Of course you're right.'

'But it's not that simple?'

She looked at him with something like gratitude and Angelo felt a chip of the reinforced concrete he'd constructed around his heart crack and fall away.

Ally's voice dipped low. 'No, it's not. The memory itself is nice, comforting even. And the way we spoke, I know we're very close.' She shot him a glance then looked away. 'After what you told

me I'd begun to wonder if there was anyone, anywhere who cared when I didn't come home.'

Another lump of reinforcing sheered away,
leaving Angelo feeling scraped raw. He had
nothing to be guilty about, he told himself. He'd
merely told her the truth about their relationship.

But he'd enjoyed it too much, hadn't he? The
chance to inflict hurt on the woman who'd hurt
him years before.

Angelo wasn't proud of himself in that moment.

'Now you know there is.' He squeezed her hand
and was relieved when she returned his grip.

'Yes.' Yet still she didn't look happy. 'The problem is that the memory made me incredibly sad.
Which makes me scared of what I'll discover
when I finally remember everything.' Her hand
clutched his. 'I'm not sure I'm ready to face that.'

CHAPTER EIGHT

'THIS IS AMAZING.' Ally stopped on the last step of the cliff path and took off her sandals, taking in the deserted cove with the deep blue sea sparkling beyond. Stepping onto the unusual pearly pink sand, she wriggled her toes. 'It's as soft as icing sugar too.'

Angelo turned and looked over his shoulder, eyebrows lifted at her delighted reaction. The twist of his body accentuated the breadth of his shoulders and the narrowness of his hips.

Instantly she forgot all about the secluded, perfect beach, her gaze feasting instead on him.

He was breathtakingly masculine. In black swim-shorts and a thin T-shirt he looked toned and taut. Ally had to drag her attention away from those heavy thigh muscles and powerful arms.

'I like it. The private beach was one of the things that attracted me to the villa.'

'It must be great, having the place to yourself.'

On a public beach Angelo would probably be mobbed by admirers.

Ally swallowed hard, telling herself she was

too aware of him as a man. It had grown worse in the last couple of days, since Angelo had dropped his antagonism and wariness.

Yesterday when she'd had her mini meltdown at the lunch table he'd been kind and understanding. He'd drawn her close and let her snuffle out her tears without making her feel in the least foolish that she didn't even know what she was crying about.

But that sadness had been piercingly raw. It had hit out of nowhere, stealing her breath and her strength and turning the bright day gloomy with despair.

She'd tried to tell herself her brain wasn't working properly. That she was imagining things. Yet the awful suspicion lingered. That when she *did* remember everything she'd wish she'd remained in ignorance. Because something awful had happened.

Since then she'd spent as much time as possible with Angelo. Being with him took her thoughts off the unknown, scary past.

Yeah, because you're busy lusting after him.

Nonsense. She was just *appreciating* him. Any woman would.

But did other women toss and turn all night, alternately wishing he were with her and dreaming that he was?

Heat scored her cheeks and Ally watched his gaze sharpen. Sometimes it felt as if Angelo read her thoughts, or at least her body's response to him.

Maybe he could. They'd been lovers.

Ally wrinkled her nose, concentrating on not shifting her weight as that edgy, needy feeling started up again at the apex of her thighs. She mightn't have any memory but she was pretty certain it was her body's way of telling her she wanted sex. With Angelo Ricci.

Which was *not* going to happen.

'So, are you going to show me where I washed up and where you found the paddle?' Her voice sounded strident with forced cheer. But better than hoarse with arousal.

'You're sure you feel like clambering over rocks? There's nothing to see now.'

Angelo had been solicitous to the point of smothering since that scene at lunch yesterday. He'd insisted she lie down until the doctor came and pronounced she was doing well. Even this morning, when Ally said she was going to the beach, he'd tried to persuade her not to.

He seemed to think she was physically fragile, whereas it was only her mind that wasn't working. Her body seemed fine.

Too fine, considering how it responded to those

delicious pheromones he exuded, and his sheer physical presence.

'Absolutely. I'd rather be outdoors. I'm not used to being cooped up. It doesn't feel right, lounging about.' She saw his sharp look and hurriedly added, 'Though I'm enjoying the books you've lent me.'

He didn't say anything, just surveyed her as if she were a puzzle to be solved. Then abruptly he nodded. 'This way.'

He led her to an outcrop of rock at one end of the beach. 'You were lying here with your head and arm on the rock and most of your body in the water.'

Ally's body iced at the image he conjured. She could almost see herself, unconscious, head just above water. She'd been lucky not to drown or be more severely injured.

'It's okay, Ally.' His low voice wrapped around her reassuringly, as did his warm fingers, covering hers where she rubbed her hands up her arms. His touch stopped the movement, drawing her eyes to his.

She read sympathy in that dark chocolate gaze. Yet it wasn't sympathy she wanted. It was desire.

She wanted Angelo to want her again, even if fleetingly. Being constantly on tenterhooks, close to him but keeping her distance, was too much to ask.

Abruptly she stepped clear of his touch and looked out across the water. She could make out buildings on the mainland, clustered around the sea and climbing the steep slopes.

'You really think I came from there?' It was too far to swim, but maybe on a paddleboard...

'It seems so. I sent that photo you let me take of you to the hire company owner. He's sure you're the woman who rented the missing board.'

Her heart thudded. A real lead then, not just supposition. Now they just had to work out where she'd come from. 'Did he say how much he's out of pocket for the loss?'

She turned to find Angelo staring at her. 'Don't worry. It's covered by insurance.'

Ally expelled a breath. One small thing less to worry about. She had plenty of big things to worry about. 'Where did you find the paddle?'

He led her further over the rocks to a place where they ran like a ragged spine out into the sea. 'There, wedged under that outcrop.'

Of course there was nothing to see now. It was days since the storm. Even so, Ally had to clamp down on disappointment.

Had she really hoped that coming here would help her remember?

'I'm sorry, Ally. The whole island is on alert for any flotsam that might have come ashore in the storm, in case there's some sort of clue. But so far there's nothing.'

Her head jerked up. 'Thank you. That's very kind.' It shouldn't surprise her, after all he'd done for her. Of course he had a vested interest in helping her retrieve her memory so she could leave. 'I suppose the paddleboard is halfway to Sicily by now.'

Understanding warmed his gaze. 'Come on. Since there's nothing more to see, let's have that swim.'

He reached out a hand and she took it, some of the tension in her upper body easing at the contact.

Ally knew the gesture was just because Angelo didn't want her tripping on the uneven rocks and further damaging herself. But any human contact was welcome.

She'd felt so alone, isolated in a claustrophobic world where she didn't belong.

Surely that was why she'd become fixated on Angelo. It was simpler to focus on her hormonal reaction to a supremely sexy man than face the grim reality of her amnesia.

Any diversion was welcome. So as soon as they were on the sand she stripped off the lightweight trousers and top she wore over her bikini and headed for the water.

From the corner of her eye she saw Angelo yank off his T-shirt and toss it on the sand with the beach towels. The sun caressed the taut, muscled lines of his frame, burnishing his olive skin so that he seemed to glow.

It reinforced that fantasy she'd had before, of him as a fallen angel, beautiful, mesmerising and untouchable.

Ally's fingers tickled as she imagined touching his firm chest, tracing a line down to his navel, then following the dark thread of hair that disappeared beneath his shorts.

Her breath hissed between her teeth and she ran into the water, barely noticing its cool caress against ankles, knees and thighs before she shallow-dived beneath the surface.

Angelo watched her rub her hair dry with a beach towel.

But it wasn't her hair he was watching. It was the effect of that vigorous movement on her body. Ally's breasts, deliciously full in that bikini top, jiggled enticingly and her taut rear shimmied when she turned.

She was even more alluring than he remembered, still slim but with fuller curves.

Yet it was her expression that dug down past his defences. Not because of sultry glances or pouting lips. Instead Ally wore a wide, open grin and the sight of it made something within him sit up and beg.

She looked radiant, her skin flushed with exertion, her eyes bright with pleasure and her hair a tangle of old gold, glinting in the sun as she dropped the towel.

'Wasn't it glorious? The water is so clear.'

'You definitely have an affinity with the sea.'

'Maybe that's why I loved it here before. You said I never left the estate.'

Slowly Angelo nodded. It was true. Yet his memories of the past were of her lounging in the shade by the pool and occasionally taking a quick dip to cool off. He didn't recall her swimming laps of the cove. Ally had only stopped when he'd reminded her of the need to take it easy or risk possible repercussions and the doctor's wrath.

People change. Obviously she's taken up new habits since she left you.

Yet it surprised him. In Angelo's mind she was fixed in time and character, unchanging from the way she'd been five years ago.

Had their destructive relationship been a catalyst for change in her too? For the first time he wondered what had made her the grasping woman she'd been when they'd met. He'd never taken time to think about that.

Because their relationship had been shallow, grounded in sex and then the fiction of her pregnancy. He hadn't probed deeper.

Now Angelo discovered he had more in common with his ex-wife than he'd had at the time of their marriage.

A love of the sea and of books for relaxation. A penchant for straight talking.

Last night, needing something to divert him from the intimacy of her company, he'd found an old classic film to watch, something he hadn't done in ages. To his surprise Ally had not only enjoyed it but commented on it knowledgably, revealing a knowledge of vintage films that led to an animated discussion.

Angelo had enjoyed the evening more than any he could remember in a long time.

Now he enjoyed watching his ex-wife dress.

He told himself to look away and he did turn to shake out his towel. But from the corner of his eye he caught the wriggle of her hips as she pulled on loose trousers. For some reason they looked particularly sexy with the shadow of her bikini bottom clearly visible through the white fabric. As for the floaty green top, it set-

tled around her, sheer and spangled and disturb-
ingly tempting, giving tantalising glimpses of
her body underneath.

'Ready?' he asked.

Another bright smile and it struck him that she
was right. She seemed happier out of doors.

'Sounds good. I thought I'd help Enzo after
lunch. The storm played havoc with the garden.
There's still a lot of raking and pruning to do and
tying things up.'

Angelo nodded, trying to get used to this new
woman who'd rather work in the garden than
sip cocktails on a lounger. He gestured for her
to precede him up the steps so he could help her
if she suddenly flagged. Though, given the way
she seemed to spark with energy today, that was
unlikely.

He realised his error when he found himself
mesmerised by the seductive sway of her hips
and the sight of her trousers clinging to her damp
bikini, giving him a perfect view of her shapely
derriere.

His body tightened and he forced himself to
stop and look away, turning his thoughts to business calls he needed to make. Work would be a
welcome diversion from this woman. There was
an issue in New York to sort and—

Voices snagged his attention and he looked up

to see Ally had stopped ahead on the bend where the track zigzagged back across the cliff. At that corner the path reached the side boundary of his property.

Loping up the stairs Angelo found Ally smiling at his neighbour, who was leaning towards her through a gap in the thick planting. She seemed rapt in what he was saying.

'Here he is now,' she said as Angelo stopped behind her. 'You can ask him yourself.'

But Oliver Branston, Angelo's new American neighbour, didn't instantly look at Angelo. Instead his gaze rested on Ally as if he too found her mesmerising.

Angelo bristled, the skin drawing tight between his shoulder blades. 'Hi.' He pasted on a smile. 'Is there something I can help with?'

Branston had only bought the property a month ago and had so far kept to himself.

'I'm having a housewarming party.' He raised a hand as if fending off objections. 'Don't worry, it's not a noisy Hollywood blow-out with strobe lights and circling helicopters. I'm just inviting some neighbours over for a barbecue. To get to know you all and maybe allay fears people might have about me being here.'

Angelo smiled, liking the guy's self-awareness. Some of the locals had worried about having their cherished peace and privacy disturbed by a man as well-known for his partying as his impressive film-making.

'Thanks. I'll look forward to it.'

It would be a good opportunity to take the man's measure.

'Excellent. The day after tomorrow, wander over any time in the evening.' Branston nodded and shifted his attention to Ally. 'You too, Miss Ally. I expect to see you there.'

With a wave he was gone, leaving Angelo to ponder the way he'd looked at Ally with obvious approval. Maybe he looked at every woman that way. If Rosetta were to be believed, the man had been romantically linked with dozens of the world's top actresses.

It didn't matter. Ally would be resting at the villa, not going to a party.

The thought settled the edginess that had stirred in Angelo's gut when he'd discovered Ally smiling up at a Hollywood heart-throb. Oliver Branston might be a director, not an actor, but with his golden good looks and movie mogul power he drew women like bees to nectar.

Angelo and Ally walked together the rest of the way, chatting about their swim and the view, and that too settled his ruffled senses.

In the old days she'd have been beside herself

with excitement after meeting Branston, given her dream of moving from modelling to acting. But Ally showed no excitement over meeting their famous neighbour.

More and more Angelo found himself liking this new version of the woman he'd known.

'There you are, Ally. A gorgeous drink for a gorgeous woman.'

Ally looked from Oliver's dancing blue eyes to the extraordinary drink he held out to her. It was outrageously decorated with four sorts of fruit, a paper umbrella and a fizzing sparkler.

A laugh bubbled in her throat at his over-the-top comment. 'You're wasted in the movies. You should be a full-time barman.'

It was the second mocktail he'd made her tonight. The doctor hadn't specifically banned alcohol but Ally didn't want anything to hinder her brain's recovery.

Yet for some reason she'd felt shy, requesting a soft drink when all around were glamorous people quaffing fine wine and cocktails.

Maybe she felt on edge because Angelo hadn't wanted her to attend the party. First he'd warned that she needed rest, though she felt fine. Then he'd insisted the doctor wouldn't approve. Thankfully the doctor had agreed that the stimulation of company might be good for her.

Ally had been growing quietly desperate with the need for something to take her mind off Angelo. Since their truce, it grew harder to rein in her attraction. A night spent with other people was a heaven-sent opportunity.

Oliver grinned. 'It's good to know I've got another career option if my next film flops.'

'As if! I looked you up. Even if it did, you'd still have backers. You've made so many great movies.'

'You had to look me up?' His eyebrows rose. 'I knew you weren't a groupie out to get a part in one of my films, but I'd sort of hoped my name was familiar.'

Ally hesitated. Her medical condition wasn't something she'd mentioned. She didn't want to seem more of an outsider than she already felt, surrounded by all these wealthy, privileged people. Some had been friendly but they'd preferred talking to people they already knew than making small talk with a stranger.

'The fact is, Oliver, I have a slight problem. My memory…'

As she briefly told him of her accident he moved closer, concern and interest on his face.

'For real? Sorry. Of course it's for real. You

wouldn't joke about anything like that.' He peered down at her, exuding a sympathy that warmed her. 'You're one gutsy woman. Coming here, acting as if everything's normal when it must be as scary as hell.'

She blinked, her eyes suddenly too hot. 'Thank you. The doctor says I'm doing well but it doesn't feel that way.'

'Aw, Ally, I'm sorry. I didn't mean to upset you.' He wrapped his arm around her shoulders and squeezed reassuringly before stepping back.

'You didn't. I mean, it is upsetting when I think about it but you didn't upset me.' She drew a slow breath. 'It's good to talk about it with someone else.'

As she spoke she felt a familiar prickling up the back of her neck and turned to discover Angelo on the far side of the wide pool deck, staring at her from under frowning brows. Again.

He'd spent most of the evening at her side, but he was popular among the guests and more than once he'd got caught up by people wanting to talk with him. Ally had been happy to wander on her own for a little and enjoy the stunning setting.

Now he didn't look supportive or understanding. He looked like a thundercloud about to burst.

'Your lover looks ready to strangle me.'

'Angelo's not my lover and he's probably angry with me, not you. Though why he's upset I don't know.'

It hurt and annoyed her. She'd thought all that was in the past.

'That's easy. He's jealous of you being with me.'

Ally stared at the American, his outrageous words jangling in her brain. When she turned back it was to see Angelo moving purposefully towards them, until an older woman with rubies at her throat and ears stopped him, her expression worried.

'Jealous?' Ally shook her head and turned back to Oliver. 'No way. There's nothing between us.'

'Obviously he wants there to be something between you.' Oliver's mouth curled into a seductive smile. 'But if you're not lovers that means there's a chance for me.'

Again he made her giggle with his over-the-top chivalry. 'You really play up the louche playboy routine, don't you?'

For a second she saw surprise in Oliver's blue eyes. Then he shrugged. 'Habit. And you *are* intriguing and beautiful.'

Suspicion stirred. 'You want something, don't you? What is it, Oliver?'

* * *

By the time Angelo extricated himself politely from his mother's friend, Ally and Oliver Branston were nowhere to be seen.

He prowled inside to the reception rooms but there was no sign of the pair. The agitation in his gut worsened.

He'd *known* he shouldn't have brought Ally here. He'd told himself it was because she still needed to recuperate. But since he'd seen her and Branston, giggling like a couple of teenagers over the cocktail he'd made her, Angelo realised it was more than that.

He didn't like the expression in Branston's eyes when he looked at Ally.

Angelo hadn't enjoyed the way *any* of the men looked at her tonight.

What had possessed Rosetta to buy that skin-tight dress in electric blue that drew every eye?

Heat circled his throat and he lifted a hand to loosen his collar, only to discover the top of his shirt was open.

'Angelo. I'm glad to see you. I wanted your opinion—'

'Sorry,' he interrupted before an acquaintance could detain him. 'I have to find my companion—'

'The lovely blonde? I don't blame you. Last

time I looked, Branston was monopolising her, leading her into the garden.'

'Thanks,' Angelo shot over his shoulder, already halfway to the French doors. 'I'll catch you later.'

His pulse beat a quick tattoo that matched his short, sharp breaths. He plunged across the terrace and into the rambling garden.

Ally loved gardens. Maybe Branston was just showing her his plants.

Yeah. And what else is he showing her?

Angelo needed to protect her.

He swallowed a growl of fury and strode down the path, noting how secluded and private the garden seemed after the chatter of guests mere metres away.

If Branston laid a finger on Ally…

The thought died as he rounded a corner and found the pair strolling together in a small courtyard. Their heads were together as if whispering secrets. As he watched, Ally stopped and Branston moved closer and took her arm.

Fury at Branston exploded in Angelo's belly.

The denotation sent shockwaves through his body, making his heart pound. What would he have found if he'd waited another twenty minutes to follow them?

He waited, breath severed, for her reaction.

But, instead of pulling back, Ally leaned into the other man and Branston's arms went around her, his head dipping towards hers.

This time it wasn't an explosion radiating out from Angelo's belly. It was a piercing stab of pain shearing from his throat, through his chest and right down to his feet, soldered to the ground.

Ally didn't need saving. She *wanted* Branston's touch.

The revelation hit like a smack to the face.

Angelo felt his lungs collapse as the air inside rushed out on an exhalation of realisation and hurt.

How could he not have suspected?

How could he not have *known*?

Suddenly everything became clear.

Amazing that he hadn't worked it out earlier.

From the first he'd understood his ex-wife would only come to the island because she expected to get something from it.

In his hubris, Angelo had assumed she was angling for a reconciliation. Then, over the last week, she'd convinced him that her amnesia was real and she was, at the moment at least, guileless and needing support.

How she'd played him.

Again.

Pain shot through his jaw and around his skull

as he ground his teeth. To be gulled by a predatory woman once was a monumental blow. To be gulled twice...

It wasn't Angelo she wanted. He'd just been a convenient tool in her latest scheme.

She'd come to the island because Branston had bought the estate adjoining Angelo's. If there was one thing she'd always wanted as much as money it was the chance to become an actress.

Her performance this week really had been superb. She'd convinced Angelo, who of all men should have known better, that she was wounded and fragile. All the while she'd been waiting for a chance to connect with the top Hollywood director who had a reputation for taking unknowns and turning them into stars.

Angelo remembered her on the cliff path two days ago, eyes wide as she'd simpered up at Branston. She must have been waiting for an opportunity to meet him.

No wonder she'd been adamant about attending the party. Now her decision to wear a dress that left little to the imagination made sense.

Except Angelo refused to be a pawn in her plans. He strode across to the pair, gravel crunching underfoot. Even then Ally didn't look up. She was too busy sinking against Branston as if she knew she only had seconds to make an impact.

'Branston, you—'

'Good thing you're here,' the other man said. 'Ally's not feeling well. I think she needs to go home.'

She does indeed, all the way to Australia. The sooner the better.

'Angelo.' Her voice had a husky throb that caught something in his chest. Except now he knew the emotion he heard was fake. Like that wide-eyed look of fragility.

For a moment he was tempted to walk away, leave her to make her play for Branston and be done with it. But he refused to make it so easy for her.

Instead he moved close, wrapped her arm through his and led her away. Branston came all the way to the front gate, obviously concerned. She'd certainly made an impact in an incredibly short time.

The realisation fuelled Angelo's fury. But he wasn't into public scenes. In silence he led her into his villa. Even then she didn't stop her act. How far would she take this pretence?

He led her upstairs, noting her earlier faltering steps had become firm and she leaned on him less.

Finally, at her suite, she opened the door and went inside, turning to face him.

Before she could speak he followed her, making her step back. 'That was quite a performance. It's almost a shame your scheme won't work.'

'Performance? I don't understand.'

Angelo crossed his arms, staring down into her bewildered face.

He hated that, even now, he was attracted to this lying woman. Supporting her back to the villa, he'd been bombarded with her scent, sweet and enticing, and he still felt the effect of her body against his.

He was aroused with an unholy combination of physical desire and fury.

Fury, not even because she wanted to use Branston to boost her career. But because she'd pressed herself against him, when it should have been *Angelo* she seduced.

Because, despite everything, Angelo still wanted her.

'Then what *do* you understand, Ally? This?'

With one long step he closed the space between them and wrapped his fingers around her wrist.

CHAPTER NINE

ALLY STARED UP into eyes so dark they looked like the midnight sky on a moonless night. No light, no softness.

Yet it wasn't softness she craved.

Her body fizzed with adrenaline from being so close to Angelo. Even this harsh Angelo who looked more like the dark angel who'd sat in judgement on her in the early days, instead of the kind, nurturing man she'd come to know.

She was torn between shock and delight. Because finally her secret craving for closeness had come true. So instead of pulling free she simply tipped her chin higher and held her ground.

'There is no scheme, Angelo. Oliver and I were talking and suddenly I felt woozy.'

It had hit out of nowhere, that sudden weakness as her legs wobbled and her brain clouded. She'd brushed against a low shrub, releasing a heady wave of scent. The next thing she knew she was faint, her pulse racing and her head turning woolly as fragments, not of memory but of emotions, bombarded her. She'd felt so much and so abruptly, it had cut her off at the knees.

'Talking? It didn't look like you were talking from where I stood.'

'You were spying on us?'

Ally frowned, trying to make sense of his *volte face*. The man who'd been so solicitous, worrying that the party might be too taxing, was nowhere to be seen. Angelo's severe expression looked as if it was cast from unforgiving metal.

'I was concerned for you. But I needn't have bothered. Stupid of me not to have realised earlier that you only came here to get close to *him*. You want him to make you a star, don't you?' Angelo's face dipped towards hers, his mouth curling in contempt. 'Were you going to sleep with him to get a role? Or was the plan to leave him dangling?'

Ally moved to smack his face, but he held her easily.

She sucked in a frantic breath, needing an outlet for her anger.

'It was *nothing* like that. In case you missed it, I'm too busy trying to remember who I am to worry about planning future career moves!'

Her chest rose and fell as outrage filled her. She tugged her hand and he released her.

Strange. She'd hated the sense that Angelo held her where he wanted her. Yet now she didn't know what to do with her hands. Almost as if she missed his touch!

'Oliver is simply a *nice man*.' Something she'd actually begun to believe Angelo might be. 'He saw I wasn't really comfortable and kept me company. Plus he was interested from a professional perspective in my amnesia, said it would make a great story premise.'

For once Ally hadn't minded talking about her predicament, especially as Oliver's interest made it seem, for a short time, more like an intellectual puzzle than a frightening disaster.

She'd been grateful for his company. Earlier she'd been fine with Angelo beside her, but when he got caught up in conversation she'd felt out of her depth among all those sophisticated people. Even wearing the only dress she had that seemed suitable for a party, she'd felt self-conscious and it was only partly due to the amount of bare skin her dress revealed.

'We both know your weakness for *nice men*, don't we, Alexa? How you like to use them to get what you want.'

On a surge of energy Ally stepped away, crossing her arms and scowling up at him. She hated being called Alexa and he knew it.

'If you mean yourself, Angelo Ricci, then you're wrong. You're not at all nice.'

'Excellent.' His smile was a baring of teeth. 'Then I don't have to feel guilty about this.'

He was in her space again, his body flush with hers, his arm looped around her back as his gleaming gaze captured hers.

Ally heard a whoosh of breath as her breasts rose on a sharp intake against his hard chest. Or was that the sound of a conflagration igniting inside her?

Heat engulfed her, flames licking higher as she absorbed the sensation of his powerful thigh muscles against hers and his torso pressing close.

She should be intimidated by his size and strength, by the fact that they stood flush against each other, with nowhere to hide.

Instead Ally revelled in it. In every glorious centimetre of arrogant masculinity crammed up against her.

The truth hit her in an instant of stunning acknowledgement.

This was what she'd craved for the past week. This and more.

She wasn't intimidated by him. Not a bit of it. She was challenged and she wasn't in the mood to back down. Or deny herself. She'd felt herself growing stronger by the day, but along with her recovery had come an ever-increasing need. For Angelo.

Ally grabbed the lapels of his jacket, tugging hard. As if that could shift him!

Yet remarkably he did move, his face lowering, centimetre by achingly slow centimetre, until his warm breath feathered her lips.

'There's no point trying to seduce me,' he rumbled. 'I know you and I'm awake to your schemes.'

Ally laughed. The sound was harsh as he reminded her of her unenviable situation. That almost everything she knew about herself came from Angelo Ricci.

But he didn't know everything. He had it wrong when he thought her attracted to Oliver Branston. It was *this* man, this darkling fallen angel who attracted her.

She was tired of feeling weak and unsure. Of letting others dictate what she should do and taking responsibility for her.

Out of nowhere, or more probably out of a week of fear, despair, fragile hope and bitter disappointment, rose a confidence born of the knowledge this man protested too much.

'You're immune to me? Is that it?'

Ally lifted one hand to the back of his neck and urged his head down.

There was no resistance, though his eyes glittered brighter.

His mouth met hers and there was a moment of stillness. Ally felt an invisible shockwave shudder through her. An amazing instant of recognition and anticipation.

A second later there was a surge of movement and she found herself pushed up against something solid. A wall? The door? She didn't care. All she cared about was that it anchored her against Angelo's tall frame as a tumult of sensations bombarded her.

His tongue slid deep, his mouth turning a kiss into an act of possession. His hands roving her taut frame, creating shudders of delight wherever he touched.

Ally rolled her head back to give him better access to her mouth, at the same time taking the offensive, kissing him with all the pent-up passion that had brewed for a week.

A week with the man who'd once been her husband.

Had they kissed like this when they'd been married? If so she wondered how she'd had the strength to walk away. It felt as if they'd been made for each other. As if they were yoked together by something so elemental it simply couldn't be denied.

Large hands clamped her hips, lifting her up so she teetered on her toes and she welcomed it, grabbing him for support. He moved in, one thigh thrust between hers so she couldn't fall.

Ally swallowed a soft, whimpering sound at the pressure of that solid thigh right there where she ached for him. She felt his hand on her bare leg, shoving her hemline higher, lifting the dress up so all that separated them was the light wool of his trouser leg and a scrap of red lace.

Angelo moved his leg, or maybe he lifted her against him. Either way, she felt the friction of lace and hard masculine muscle against that damp place between her thighs.

Lightning forked through the darkness behind her closed eyes. She juddered and would have gasped except Angelo swallowed the sound. He took her mouth with an insistent eroticism that turned their kiss into something new. Something that undid any last restraints her overloaded brain might have harboured.

Strong hands urged her up and she followed eagerly, pressing herself against his thigh, questing for more. If only she could get higher, to the source of all that wonderful masculine heat.

She dropped one hand from his shoulder, zeroing in on that rigid shaft of arousal.

Instantly Angelo stopped her. She thought he'd tug her grasping fingers away. But as she rose against him again, a low keening sound emerging from her throat, he froze, holding her hand against all that potent promise.

It was too much and nowhere near enough. Ally's thoughts fogged, especially when he insinuated his other hand behind her, dragging her higher and closer. Until suddenly her hips were bucking in uncontrolled movements and fire burst in her veins.

Ally shuddered with it, hot and cold. Shattering in a bright explosion of colour and sensation such as she'd never known.

She screamed, but the only sound was a muffled echo as Angelo took her ecstatic cry into himself as he kissed her.

That kiss felt...tender. Intimate.

That undid something within her, leaving her wide open and wondering.

For a suspended moment Ally was on the world's pinnacle, shimmering with delight. Then she fell, collapsing into nothingness.

It might have been a mere second later or long minutes, but when she came back to the real world she was in Angelo's arms and she'd never felt so good. Her face was pressed against his soft jacket and unyielding chest. His scent, tangy and enticing, surrounded her and she felt the strong pulse of his heart beneath her ear.

It felt strange, cradled in a man's arms. So

strange she wondered if she'd ever experienced it before. Every nerve-ending tingled with delight at the feel of Angelo's powerful arms holding her close.

Dimly she remembered she should be furious with him for his accusations. But Ally had no interest in anger, not given the indescribable, blistering joy she'd experienced. There'd be time later to talk sensibly. For now she wanted more of what she'd just had. She felt floaty with delight as if she'd never before experienced sexual pleasure.

'What's so funny?'

Intriguing how Angelo's voice rumbled out from beneath her ear.

She shook her head, not wanting to get caught up explaining that this felt like an utterly new experience and it had blown her mind.

He studied her face, his eyes shining with something that made her already softened muscles turn to mush.

Angelo turned with her in his arms then lowered her to the bed, following her down. Ally's brain atrophied as his long, athletic body covered hers. He nudged her knees apart and sank between them, his erection pressed intimately at the juncture of her legs and up her belly.

Were all men so big when aroused? Her heart

fluttered as if in trepidation, yet at the same time her fingers gripped his backside, eagerly drawing him towards her as her pelvis tilted up.

Angelo murmured something low and heartfelt in Italian, then, before she could stop him, lifted himself away, supporting himself on hands and knees.

Their breaths mingled as their gazes locked. With his body blocking the lamplight, Ally couldn't read his expression, but she sensed his taut control and read his heavy breathing.

'You want me,' she whispered, not sure if it was a challenge or an invitation.

'I shouldn't.'

'Nor should I want you after the way you insult me.'

Did he stiffen? 'But you do.'

Angelo's voice dropped to a deep scrape of sound that made her skin prickle all over and her nipples pucker. It was all she could do not to drag him down on top of her so she could rub herself against him.

How could she want him now when she'd just climaxed so hard she might have blacked out for a second? Was that normal?

'Don't you, Ally?'

Was it childish to clamp her lips shut rather

than admit the words? After all, he hadn't admitted it either.

Then one large hand drifted down to her breast, so soft at first she couldn't believe it, until he cupped her harder, his thumb brushing her nipple through her dress, and her whole body jolted.

'Or are you too scared to say it out loud?'

Ally refused to let him feel superior. She lifted her hand, stroking the straining fabric that covered his thigh, then covered his erection with her palm.

Angelo's hissed breath was magic, as was the sudden shudder of his body.

'And you want *me*, Angelo. This is mutual. Stop pretending you're not interested.'

Above her he shook his head, his expression bordering on incredulous. 'Not interested? You've been driving me out of my mind ever since you washed up on my beach.'

At last. Honesty. Honesty and desire.

Ally felt something take off inside her, as if a flock of birds had risen from a tree and soared into the bright sky.

'Good.' Her voice was husky, only just audible. 'Because you've been doing the same to me.'

There was such freedom in admitting it. Not holding herself in any longer.

For a moment longer they remained unmoving, yet it felt as if everything shifted, the world turning over like a giant kaleidoscope and locking into a new, unfamiliar pattern.

'Hold that thought.'

Angelo crawled backwards, down the bed. He shouldered his way out of his jacket and reached for her feet, slipping off first one sandal then the other.

It was a simple thing. It shouldn't be erotic at all, but Angelo took the time to massage her instep and Ally had to bite back a moan of delight as her eyes closed and she gave herself up to sensual pleasure. This man knew his way around a woman's erogenous zones. She could barely believe she'd climaxed against him while they were still fully clothed and now she was blissing out from the touch of his hands on her feet.

Finally he skimmed those clever hands up her bare legs, so slowly that her breath came in tortured gasps as she waited for him to reach the edge of her short dress. Soon he was pushing it higher, and she shifted her hips so he could free the material.

Callused hands caught the narrow lace at her hips and rolled it down, lower and lower, finally drawing her panties off her feet.

Yet he didn't return to lie over her. Ally finally

opened her eyes to see him drop and settle with his shoulders between her thighs.

The sight was…arresting. Incredibly erotic, especially when he sensed her regard and lifted his head to meet her stare. Something passed between them, hot and hectic, and Ally felt her heartbeat pound against her ribs and lower, between her legs.

Angelo's mouth curved up in a smile that melded desire with greed. As if he wanted to taste her there. The idea made her quiver in arousal.

'Angelo—'

'It's okay. I'll take care of you.' He was already lowering his head when Ally leaned up, putting out her hand to stop him.

'No! I don't want that.'

Glittering eyes met hers and she read surprise in his pared-back features.

Exciting as it was, seeing him there, Ally wanted something else. Next time she exploded in ecstasy she wanted to be *with Angelo*, not alone.

She needed him desperately.

'I want *you.*'

Ridiculous to feel heat scorch her throat and cheeks. They must have had sex lots of times and, from what Angelo hinted, she wasn't shy. But Ally felt shy now, lying with her legs sprawled wide and Angelo there between them. Shy as she hadn't felt when she'd climaxed against him.

'Please, Angelo.'

Ally had no doubt that Angelo would make it good for her. He was experienced and obviously knew how to please her. Yet she could only go with her instinct. She wanted them, together. To lose herself in his arms.

A sigh of relief eased from her lungs as he reared back and, holding her eyes, hauled off his shirt.

Ally's gaze flickered to his straight shoulders and down the leanly sculpted chest she'd so admired when they'd swum together. He really was stunning. How would it feel when they came together, naked?

'Take your dress off, Ally. Or do you want me to do it?'

For answer she scrambled to sit up and reached for the zip at her back. Her tongue was stuck to the roof of her mouth. She doubted she could speak anyway, not when Angelo was unbuckling his belt and reaching for his zip, every movement slow and methodical, in contrast to the movements of her damp, fumbling fingers.

In the end she had to sit up and pull the fastening around to her side so she could see where she'd caught fabric in the teeth of the zip. Finally she dragged the zip down and shoved the dress low, wriggling to get out of it.

That was when she remembered she was braless, as her breasts swung free and she heard an intake of breath.

A deep voice murmured, 'Don't stop there.'

Angelo felt the air back up in his lungs as he surveyed her, dishevelled, rosy-cheeked and heart-stoppingly alluring. For a second she looked as if she contemplated pulling the dress back up to cover herself. But as her eyes met his, Ally's expression morphed into one of excitement.

He felt the heavy drag of her stare as it dropped from his face, down his body to his sheathed penis. His erection pulsed in response to that hungry stare and he almost chuckled at her look of surprise.

A tiny part of his brain puzzled over Ally's reactions. The way she'd stopped him going down on her was new. The shock he read now on her face. Was it possible he'd been wrong? Maybe she really did have amnesia.

Maybe he was mistaken about her and Oliver. Had he allowed his bias against her, not to mention plain, old-fashioned jealousy, colour his perceptions?

Angelo didn't have enough brainpower to puzzle it out now. His mind was fixed on Ally shimmying out of that slinky blue dress, her breasts bobbing enticingly.

His breath sheared off as she dragged the material lower. The contrast between plump, rose-tipped breasts and her narrow waist dried his mouth. Then the gentle curve out to her hips…

The years had changed her, filled out her curves a little more, but he liked that. The thatch of dark blonde hair between her thighs had surprised him. She'd always been bare there, ready for her bikini modelling. But he liked the natural look. Even the unfamiliar way she blushed appealed, enhancing the feeling that this was special and new.

Angelo swallowed hard. It was only as the dress fell to the floor that he found his voice again. 'You're even more beautiful than I remember.'

Stunning eyes the colour of a dusk sky met his. Electricity zapped across his skin and arrowed to his heavy groin. She swallowed, like him teetering on the brink.

He kept his eyes locked on hers as he prowled up the bed. He was already so aroused he didn't trust himself to survey her lovely body again.

Angelo paused above her, swallowing air that tasted of Ally, sweet and hot. He shuddered, too aware that any incidental touch might send him over the edge.

'Ready?'

She nodded, her eyes huge and brilliant, and he felt himself sinking into them like a man without a life raft.

He wasn't sure if he was reassuring her or himself as he cupped her cheek and watched her gaze soften. All he knew was that this was different. He'd thought he'd known this woman so well, but now, despite the past, this moment felt unique. He couldn't remember ever being so close to losing control so quickly.

Angelo shook his head, pushing the thought away as he focused on the mechanics of bringing them both the utmost pleasure without spilling himself prematurely. It was a problem he hadn't had since his teens but he was so aroused this was going to be tough. Wonderful but tough.

'Relax,' he murmured, bending to brush his mouth across hers. As he did she sighed and reached up to clasp the back of his neck with both hands as if claiming him for herself.

The idea appealed, as did the husky little murmurs she made as he kissed the corners of her mouth.

Ally tugged at his neck, trying to bring him

closer, and he obliged, covering her delicious body with his own.

For a second they were both absolutely still, absorbing each new sensation. Angelo felt a shudder begin in his groin, race through his buttocks and all the way up his spine to make his nape tingle and tighten.

'You feel so good,' he growled against her mouth.

'So do you.' She shifted beneath him and he sank deeper between her thighs, heat meeting heat.

Suddenly Angelo couldn't wait any longer, despite his best intentions to take his time.

Kneeing her thighs wider, he stroked her breast and felt her quiver. He kissed her there, feeling her move needily beneath his mouth as he slid his hand between her legs. Gently he explored, finding that tiny nub, smiling against her breast as she tensed beneath him.

He explored further, deeper, and she responded with a rise of her hips that spoke of an urgency that matched his.

No more foreplay. Not when they were both so needy.

Lifting his head so he could watch Ally's expression, he hooked one of her slender legs over his hip and positioned himself. Her eyes weren't wide now. They were slitted and slumbrous, pure invitation.

Angelo smiled as he tilted his hips and pushed.

It was all he could have hoped for and more. Ally's expression, the soft embrace of her body, that searing, close heat enfolding him. He felt like some conquering hero about to claim the world's greatest prize.

Angelo gave himself up to beckoning bliss and thrust, hard and smooth, into paradise. Only to freeze, a split second too late, as he felt a barrier that was there one moment then gone the next.

Ally stiffened, her lovely, limber body turning rigid.

Stunned, he looked down into wide eyes and a mouth drawn back in pain. He saw her pulse pound frantically, felt her fingernails dig into his shoulders as a great tremor passed through her.

Some part of his brain was still working, trying to tell him something. But it couldn't be.

Yet, as Ally's eyes welled with unshed tears and she gulped in a shuddery gasp of hurt, he realised it was true.

Ally was a virgin!

CHAPTER TEN

THROUGH A HAZE of shock, Ally saw Angelo frown and felt him pull back.

'Stop! Don't move!'

She clutched at his shoulders and tried to hold him to her.

The pain was starting to ease. She drew an unsteady breath, grateful for Angelo's stillness as her body adjusted to this strange new sensation.

Ally's brow crinkled. How could it feel that way when they'd done this before, and when she'd wanted it so badly? Even if she hadn't been sexually active for a while, surely it wouldn't feel like this.

The answer was obvious but too perplexing to take in now. For, as she relaxed a little under his weight, the uncomfortable tightness changed to anticipation.

Ally would make sense of it later. For now what she wanted, *needed*, was the pleasure that had beckoned so brightly.

She drew a deep breath that didn't seem to fill her cramped lungs. 'You can move now.'

To her consternation, Angelo withdrew totally, leaving her bereft.

'Not like that,' she gasped.

'What do you want, Ally?'

He spoke through gritted teeth, the tendons in his neck standing proud and his features stark, as if his skin had shrunk. He looked like she'd felt a second ago, hurting and holding it in.

'I want you, Angelo. Please don't stop.'

He was shaking his head before she finished. 'We can't. You're not—'

'None of that matters. I want you, Angelo.' She swallowed the last of her pride as she reached for him. 'I *need* you. Don't leave me like this.'

Troubled dark eyes held hers for the longest time. Until finally, with a guttural whisper of something she couldn't catch, he knelt over her again.

Wide shoulders blocked off the room as the heat of his body blanketed her, but she kept her eyes on his, willing him on. His touch was light, each movement careful, so that when he took her again it was in slow motion, allowing her to absorb and revel in each incredible sensation. On and on it went, till Angelo and she lay together as one.

This time it felt amazing.

'No pain?' His voice was gruff.

'None at all.' She frowned, trying to find the words. 'It feels strange but not bad.'

Angelo grimaced, his laugh tight, and she realised he was probably used to more whole-hearted compliments.

'I'm sorry, I didn't mean—'

'Don't be sorry. You're being truthful. That's what matters.'

Ally saw that he meant it. Despite the grim look on his face and the aura of ruthlessly shackled energy that she supposed came from holding back. For her.

It was a reminder that he'd already given her one release but he'd had none. As simple as that, she discovered that she wanted to give him pleasure as much as she wanted it for herself.

Ally smiled up into that serious face, smoothed her hands over his shoulders and tugged him closer.

'Make love to me, Angelo. Please.'

What came next was a revelation. That a man so large and powerful could be so tender and careful shouldn't surprise her, yet again and again Ally found herself stunned by his consideration. And his capacity for discovering erogenous zones she hadn't known existed.

His every movement was slow and deliberate, calculated to delight.

It wasn't just what Angelo *did* either. The very act of holding him close thrilled her. So did the occasionally harsh sound of his breathing and his sighs of approval as she discovered some of the places where he was sensitive.

Inhaling his scent, rich with citrus, pepper and cedar, excited her. As did the taste of his skin. Ally couldn't get enough of him, kissing, licking, even nipping gently with her teeth, to be rewarded with the sight and feel of this big, powerful man shuddering with pleasure.

When he moved inside her it seemed as if the world shifted too, so profound and amazing were the sensations Angelo evoked.

Until suddenly she was clinging to him, panting for breath, feeling the rise of something inside that was both inevitable and all-consuming.

'Come for me, *cara.*'

Angelo's words caressed her cheek before he gently bit down on her earlobe, and suddenly she was arching her back, matching his rhythm with a desperation that wiped everything from her mind.

'Angelo!'

Her voice was a broken cry as she convulsed around him.

A second later, as if he'd been waiting for her,

his movements altered. The slow, easy glide becoming a charged drive into pleasure.

They clung, bodies striving, as the world burst apart and enveloped her in bliss. She'd experienced sexual release a short time ago but this was more intense, more profound, and far more than she'd expected.

When Ally came back to herself she was wrapped in Angelo's arms, his head in the curve of her neck, his breath humid on her flesh and his chest heaving. She loved the feel of him slumped there and wrapped her arms around him. Her heart was pounding and so was his. She felt it hammering behind his ribs.

A moment later he muttered something in a low, voiceless rumble and lifted himself off her.

Ally couldn't stop a muffled protest at the idea of him moving away. At least he only rolled onto his back beside her, his body touching hers all the way down her side.

She drew a shaky breath and tried to comprehend what had just happened. It had been stunning, not just physically but emotionally. Instinctively she shied from examining her feelings too closely because she feared what they might reveal.

She was groping for something to say when

Angelo levered himself up from the bed and strode into the en suite bathroom without a word.

Ally frowned. But what had she expected? Kind words?

It had been sex, pure and simple. They'd goaded each other into it, angry as well as sexually aroused. It would be a mistake to read anything more into what had happened.

Yet she recalled Angelo's expression as he'd joined with her the second time. The patience and care he'd shown. More than that, she'd felt real tenderness, almost reverence.

Could it be that, despite the circumstances, they had found something special? It *felt* as if they'd shared something that transcended simple carnal lust.

But what did she know? She'd been a virgin.

The knowledge was like an earthquake, undermining the few certainties she'd managed to cobble together. If she'd been a virgin then surely that meant she wasn't the woman Angelo believed her.

Where did that leave her?

Who was she?

Suddenly fear stirred. Fear of being adrift again. Of that grey world of nothingness that had engulfed her when she'd first woken to no memory.

* * *

Angelo planted his palms on the marble benchtop and stared at himself in the mirror. He looked the same as usual but he felt completely different. As if the world had tilted on its side and everything he knew or thought he knew had shattered.

His body still pulsed from orgasm and his brain was foggy from the remnants of explosive ecstasy, but his belly roiled with a sickening mix of guilt, shock and awe. It felt selfish to dwell on how wonderful their sexual encounter had been when the implications were so mighty, turning everything upside down.

How badly had he hurt her? His gut clenched as he recalled her stunned gaze, eyes wide and pleading.

How had he got everything totally wrong?

He squeezed his eyes shut, trying to identify a moment when he might have withdrawn and walked away from tonight's tempestuous events. But there wasn't one. Making love to Ally had been inevitable from the moment they'd marched into her room, sparking fire off each other.

No, earlier than that. From the moment he'd seen her with Oliver and rage had boiled in his blood along with jealousy. It had already been too late then.

As it had been even earlier in the evening. From

the moment she'd sashayed into the living room in that slinky blue dress and something inside his brain had shorted. He'd tried and failed to keep her away from the party because he'd known the alternative, spending the night at home, trying to ignore how much he wanted her, was inconceivable.

Angelo tried to comfort himself with the knowledge that what had happened had been mutual. She'd wanted him as much as he'd wanted her.

Want. Such a weak word for that tremendous surge of desire, possessiveness and sheer desperation.

He hung his head. It didn't matter how fated it had seemed. Or that they'd both been desperate for it.

He'd just deflowered a virgin.

An innocent.

Not his ex-wife. Not a woman who understood that, however compelling their drive for intimacy, this wasn't about love but about raw, unvarnished lust.

Ally wasn't the woman he'd believed her. Yet she'd had to withstand his withering scorn. He shrank at the memory of how he'd treated her since her arrival, taking his anger out on her.

This wasn't Alexa but a woman he didn't know. A woman who didn't know him.

He might not have seduced her into sex. It had been entirely mutual. Yet that didn't stop his guilt. It tormented him, curdling his stomach. He should have been caring for her, not giving in to lust.

His mother and sister told him he was over-protective, shouldering too much responsibility and trying to safeguard them from every hurt. Maybe they were right. But tonight, again, he'd failed spectacularly as a protector.

Angelo raked a hand through his hair and straightened, sucking in a deep breath.

It was time to see how Ally was.

He paused in the doorway to the bedroom, heart slamming into his ribs as he saw her lying, curled on her side, looking spent and fragile.

How badly had he hurt her? The question made him feel queasy, but he had to know.

He crossed the room and gingerly sank onto the bed beside her. She didn't look up, though she must have felt the mattress sink.

She was shivering and he reached out to drag a cover over her nakedness, then paused, notic-ing the small but tell-tale smudge of colour on the bed behind her.

Angelo's heart shrank.

He should have followed his instincts there and then and got right away from her. But when she'd looked at him with those big eyes, wide and pleading, he hadn't been able to turn away.

Because you didn't really want to leave.

Because being with Ally felt essential to him.

'Ally? Talk to me.'

He heard a muffled sniff and brushed her hair back from her face. Relief filled him when he saw she wasn't crying, but that didn't ameliorate his guilt.

'Are you hurting? What can I do?'

Finally she turned her head to look at him. 'No. I'm okay.'

'You don't look it.'

He was used to lovers who sighed and snuggled and talked about next time. By contrast Ally looked strained and pale, but who could blame her?

A gurgle of laughter surprised him and her mouth tilted up into a tiny smile. 'Thanks for the compliment. Just what a woman wants to hear.'

'You're shivering. Of course I'm concerned.' His mouth firmed. 'I hurt you. I can't tell you how sorry I am. If I'd known—'

'You didn't know. Neither of us did.'

Angelo shook his head. 'I should have realised. I can't believe I didn't work it out before.'

Yet, as he said it, he marvelled at how much this woman looked like his ex-wife. The bone structure, the shape of her mouth and nose, even her gestures. And those memorable eyes. How rare was that colour? He'd never seen the like anywhere else.

They could have been twins. Except Alexa had said she was an only child. That was one of the reasons he'd been so sure of Ally's identity.

Sure, but wrong.

'I must be very like her.'

Ally might have read his mind. Her expression as unreadable, yet Angelo heard a wealth of emotion behind her words. Silently he nodded. What could he say?

Angelo stroked Ally's hair off her face, filled with tenderness and regret for the hurt he'd caused. But not for the actual deed. He still couldn't regret that.

'Did I hurt you very much? How are you now?' He'd never been with a virgin.

She shrugged. 'It only hurt a little.' Her gaze avoided his, making him wonder. 'I'm okay now.'

Angelo wished he could believe her. 'If I'd known I would have been more careful.' What was he thinking? 'If I'd known I would never have touched you.'

At least he *hoped* he'd have been strong enough to keep his distance. But he'd never before been so devoured by passion. It made him uneasy, doubting his willpower. No other woman had ever threatened his control in this way.

'Don't!'

In a flurry of movement, Ally pushed his hand away and scrabbled further up the bed, reaching for the bed covering in a bid to conceal herself.

Angelo rose enough for her to pull the cover up then sat again, eyeing her warily. He shouldn't be surprised at her impulse for modesty, yet it felt like she was shutting him out.

Who could blame her?

'Ally, I'm sorry.'

'Stop saying that!' Her mouth tightened. 'There's nothing to be sorry about.'

She paused to draw a deep breath and Angelo forced himself not to follow the rise of her breasts beneath their thin cover.

'There's no harm done. It was just sex. Millions of people do it all the time. You used protection so there won't be consequences.' Yet Ally's voice was clipped and her shrug looked anything but insouciant. Angelo read tension in the movement. 'And if it wasn't as good for you as it usually is…' another lift of tight shoulders '… I'm sure you'll get over it.'

Angelo frowned at her. 'Not as good as usual?'

He reeled. Her dismissive *just sex* comment had

thrown him, and now she implied what they'd shared was substandard.

Ally turned away, but Angelo was so close it was hard to avoid looking at him. Plus he was naked, sitting there unfazed by his lack of clothes, while her stupid pulse pattered faster and her insides turned to mush all over again.

Given his magnificent body it wasn't surprising that he was comfortable naked. More comfortable than she was. He'd probably had plenty of lovers too, considering his charisma and good looks. And given his obvious expertise in pleasing a woman.

Ally shivered and tried to rein her wayward thoughts back in, away from the memory of him using his mouth, hands and toned, virile body to bring her to ecstasy.

'Ally, I—'

'No. Please.' She lifted her palm. 'Don't apologise again.'

She didn't think she could cope with him saying sorry any more, reinforcing how much he regretted their spur-of-the-moment coupling.

She'd already had time to work out that Angelo had been driven by fury at what he'd believed to be his ex-wife's scheming and now he thoroughly regretted what had been, for her, an amazing experience. He'd shot out of bed without a word.

'I wasn't going to apologise.'

Was that impatience in his voice? She met his eyes then looked away again, horrified by the fluttering feeling in her chest. Just the sight of him undid her.

'Good. I think—'

'I was going to say that what we just shared was anything but disappointing. It was fantastic.'

As if tugged by an invisible string, her head turned towards him. Did he mean it? She wanted to think so, but she couldn't tell if his words were just to reassure her. He met her stare easily, but what did that prove?

'I'm glad you think so,' she said carefully.

'Of course I do.' He leaned closer, his expression earnest. 'It was…spectacular.'

It sure was. For her, at least.

But she couldn't shake the idea that Angelo tried too hard to reassure her. He'd climaxed but, on a scale of one to ten, could intercourse with an inexperienced virgin compete with hot sex with someone who matched him for sensual experience?

Someone like his ex-wife.

The woman he'd thought he was bedding.

The woman, Ally realised, with a sick feeling

in her middle, he still desired, despite what had passed between them.

That was why his emotions had been roused tonight, fuelled by his unwilling attraction for the woman who'd betrayed him. The woman he still wanted. He'd been jealous, imagining her with Oliver.

That explained his sudden and complete withdrawal when he'd discovered she wasn't Alexa. He'd only kept going because Ally had pleaded with him. Fierce heat swamped her at the thought. Pity sex, they called it.

'So, we've sorted that out. It was very nice and now it's over.'

One large hand reached out and captured hers, planting it, palm down, on his bare thigh. Ally felt the furnace heat of his body, the twitch of powerful muscle and the tickle of dark hair under her hand. It sent some signal to her brain which immediately stirred her crazy hormones back into action.

As if, having had her once, Angelo might be interested in more!

Ally kept her gaze down, not wanting him to read her thoughts. Until she realised her attention had strayed to his groin. She swallowed. No wonder there'd been pain. Angelo wasn't a little man in any respect.

'Far more than *very nice*, Ally.' His deep voice slid across her body's pleasure points, making her skin tighten and her nipples peak.

Horrified, she looked up and met his dark stare. This couldn't go on. She had to pull herself together.

She nodded, as if everything was clear and easy. 'And now it's finished. Time to move on.'

Ally watched his black eyebrows climb, as if in surprise. But there was no going back. She had to begin as she meant to go on. Not as a victim, or an object of sympathy.

'So, Angelo, the million-dollar question is, if I'm not your ex-wife, Alexa Barrett, who am I?'

CHAPTER ELEVEN

'I WISH I KNEW.'

Angelo hated seeing the pain and confusion in her beautiful shadowed eyes. Just as he hated that perfunctory tilt of her chin and her cool tone as she spoke dismissively about sex being over.

Of course it's over. She's out of bounds. She should have been out of bounds from the first.

Yet he felt dazed by the most memorable love-making of his life. He told himself that was an exaggeration but didn't believe it.

Clearly it hadn't been the same for Ally.

It had been no tender seduction. In the beginning it had been too hot and fast for an innocent. When he'd learned the truth, he'd belatedly done everything he could to make up for the initial pain. He'd thought he'd succeeded. But maybe, despite her orgasm, the whole event had been too traumatic.

If he'd known, he'd have taken more care.

If he'd known, he'd have found a way to resist her!

'We'll find out who you are.' He leaned close, aiming to reassure. 'Trust me. I have the resources to help. We'll discover your identity, you'll see.'

For the longest moment her lavender gaze locked on his and he'd have given half his fortune to know what she thought.

Was it possible that, despite the shock of what had just happened, she too felt the connection he did? Even now he felt it, more strongly than anything he'd experienced with Alexa.

Finally she nodded. 'I hope so. It's rather tough, not knowing who you are.'

Angelo's heart went out to her. There she sat, clutching the bedclothes and, if he wasn't mistaken, trying not to shiver, but downplaying her shock. She was so gallant. She gave him a lesson in true courage.

'On the upside,' he offered, trying to match her light tone, 'at least you're not my ex-wife.'

Was it selfish to be glad she wasn't the woman he'd learned to despise?

Ally laughed aloud, the sound pulling his lips into an answering smile. 'You're right. Every time you spoke about her it was to reveal something awful. I was on tenterhooks all the time, wondering what dreadful thing you were going to tell me next.' She snuggled lower into the bed. 'It's a relief to know that wasn't my life.'

Again, Angelo admired her attitude. Ally was strong, forthright and refreshing.

She needed help and he needed to begin thinking with his mind not his libido. Even if some greedy part of him wanted her to reach out to him for reassurance now everything they thought they'd known about her was disproven.

Angelo stilled at the realisation of his selfishness. No, it was far better that she was confident, even though he sensed some of what she projected was a façade.

'You said you felt suddenly woozy at the party.' It wasn't a word he was familiar with but from the context he guessed she meant unwell. 'But you were okay by the time we got back here.' He paused, thinking of how much more than simply *okay* she'd been. 'Is there anything else I need to know? Should I call the doctor?'

She shook her head, her rumpled hair sliding around her bare skin like a curtain of dark honey.

'No, it's nothing like that. I think it was a memory, or part of one.'

Yet, instead of being excited, Ally's expression grew tense. That wasn't a good sign.

'Do you want to tell me about it?'

'There's nothing much to tell. It was confused and more about feelings than a recollection of an actual event.'

'And it made you feel sick?'

Angelo's belly hollowed. Was her past so bad it affected her like that? The doctor had mentioned the possibility she'd suffered some recent trauma and that was part of the reason her brain refused to remember, as a defence against something it didn't want to face.

Ally gnawed at the corner of her mouth. She looked vulnerable, her veneer of confidence slipping. Angelo wanted to pull her to him and assure her everything would be all right, but he held back. He had no right to touch her without an invitation, no matter how much he wanted to.

'It made me feel…' She shook her head. 'Upset. But I don't know why.'

Angelo heard the fear in her voice. He could barely imagine how it would feel to have no knowledge of yourself or your past. 'Don't read too much into that. It's a big thing, regaining your memory. It's bound to knock you off-balance.'

He just hoped the doctor was wrong and she wouldn't have to face past trauma on top of all she'd already been through.

'You're right.' She scrunched up her nose in that cute way she had, then sent him a swift sideways glance. 'Despite what just happened—' she gestured to the bed '—I suppose there's no way I *could* be her?'

'Absolutely not.'

Ally mightn't know much about how sex felt but there'd been no mistaking her virginity. He almost told her about the bloodstained bedding but wondered if it might embarrass her.

'Which means I really do look like Alexa.' She shook her head. 'It seems too fantastic to be real.'

'I know what you mean.' That was why he'd been so convinced of her identity, despite the couple of differences he'd put down to time or an imperfect memory. 'But the likeness is uncanny.'

An idea occurred and Angelo shot to his feet. It only took a minute to grab his phone from his discarded trousers. He sat down again beside Ally and started searching. 'I'll show you.'

'You kept her photo?'

Ally's voice held a note he couldn't interpret.

'No.' He'd eradicated every trace of Alexa from his life. He didn't want reminders of his worst ever mistake. 'But I can find one. There.'

After a short media search he held out his phone.

Ally took it gingerly and he heard her indrawn breath.

'She's stunning!'

Angelo leaned over to look again at the photo, snapped by a press photographer as he and Alexa entered a red-carpet event in Rome. She wore a shiny sheath dress of deep purple that hung from one shoulder. It hugged her body and the long slit up the side of the skirt revealed most of one slim leg.

'She looks exactly like you.'

'I don't look like that!'

Something in Ally's voice made him look up from the phone. 'Your hair is a few shades darker and done differently.'

Ally shook her head. 'The features are very similar but she's glamorous and so incredibly poised.'

Angelo stared. 'Did you look in the mirror tonight? You're every bit as stunning. More so because it's all natural, not contrived for effect.'

His voice hit a rocky note as he remembered Ally appearing at the head of the stairs looking utterly gorgeous. She'd stolen his breath and set desire pounding through him so hard he'd tried every excuse to make her stay here in the villa.

And didn't that work out well?

That thought gave him the strength to look away when Ally stared at him wonderingly. Needing distraction, he took the phone and searched for another photo.

'Do you have wedding photos?'

Angelo flinched. 'No.' Hearing how brusque his voice was, he searched for something to soften the denial. 'It was a private wedding, with only my mother and sister as witnesses. With a baby supposedly on the way there seemed no reason to wait and Alexa said she preferred a simple ceremony.' Because she'd wanted to hook him as quickly as possible. 'Here's another.'

He passed the phone back and couldn't help noticing the brush of Ally's fingers on his.

He made himself focus on the photo. This one was of Alexa alone, modelling the sort of swimsuit designed never to get wet.

'You're right.' He couldn't tell if Ally sounded deflated or just tired. 'We're very similar, though I think we're a couple of dress sizes different.'

Angelo bit back the urge to say he much preferred her feminine curves to Alexa's thinner body. But he'd made enough mistakes for one night.

'And look at this.' Ally expanded the photo. 'Here.' She leaned, in peering over the phone and expanding the photo.

'What is it?' He saw nothing but an expanse of lean hip.

'There's no scar.'

Angelo frowned. 'Alexa never had a scar there.'

'Exactly.'

Ally thrust the phone at him and pulled aside the bedding to reveal her upper thigh and the curve of her hip. Angelo's mouth dried as he recalled the satiny texture of her skin and the sweet woman and spice scent of her body. Desire thundered through him and his hand tightened around the phone.

As he watched she tilted her body and there, on her hip, was a thin silvery scar he hadn't noticed earlier.

Because his mind had been on other things.

'More proof that you're not her.' As if any were needed. 'It doesn't look new.'

'No, I've had it for as long as I remember. Gran said I fell off a swing...' Ally's voice petered out and before his eyes her face paled, the sprinkling of freckles suddenly standing out across her nose.

Ally's hand went to her throat in an unmistakably defensive gesture.

'Are you okay?'

'I...' She shook her head, frowning. 'I remember, *almost* remember, her voice. My gran's voice.' She blinked and raised drowned eyes. 'I should be excited but it all feels wrong somehow.'

She swallowed hard, as if forcing down a lump in her throat. Angelo clenched his hands, knowing better than to reach for her.

'What can I do, Ally? How can I help?'

For several seconds she didn't answer. Finally she spoke, her voice strained. 'Would you mind just holding me? I feel cold inside and I know it's stupid because nothing's really changed, but I feel so alone.'

'Of course.'

Angelo felt as if a piece of his heart had broken away, listening to her hesitant request. After all she'd been through it was no wonder she needed comfort. He leaned over and put his phone on the bedside table.

But instead of leaning into his embrace Ally slid down under the covers. That was when he realised her teeth were chattering. Not from the temperature in the room but from shock.

He grabbed his discarded boxers, because there was no way he'd dare share a bed with her naked. Then he pulled back the bedclothes and slipped in beside her.

Instantly Ally turned onto her side and he gathered her close, her head on his shoulder, her hair tickling his chest and her bare, beautiful body flush against him.

Angelo wrapped his arms around her in a loose embrace. 'Rest now. Everything will look better in the morning. I promise.'

She nodded and he caught her sweet woman scent. It was pure temptation. But this time Angelo conquered his urge for more. Because Ally's needs came first.

* * *

Ally woke to delicious warmth. She lay on her side with her knees bent and Angelo behind her, his arm heavy across her waist, heat radiating from him.

She breathed deep, luxuriating in the feel of them lying together.

'You're awake.'

His deep voice wrapped around her like his embrace. She felt the sound rumble through his body into hers and bit her lip as familiar, needy excitement stirred.

Just like that.

She'd gone to sleep grateful for simple human contact but in an instant she was aroused by this man. A coil of heat circled low in her body and her breasts felt fuller at the thought of what they'd done together and might do again.

Ally tried to tell herself it was because he was her only lover.

Yet surely it wasn't so simple. She'd wanted Angelo from the first. Even when they were at daggers drawn there'd been a sizzling undercurrent of awareness, urging her to challenge him if she couldn't understand him.

That sexual awareness hadn't changed, even if her pride insisted she should distance herself. Because he'd bedded her thinking she was someone else. Common sense told her any attraction he felt for her was because she looked like the woman who still, obviously, evoked incredibly strong responses in him.

Ally gulped down a hot tangle of emotions and dragged in a breath that felt like shards of glass in her tight chest. Forcing her eyelids up, she was amazed to see bright daylight outside.

'You stayed all night?' She half turned, looking over her shoulder and meeting his enigmatic dark stare.

'You needed me.' The simple statement made her greedy heart tumble. 'I didn't like to leave in case I woke you.'

Unlike his hot body, Angelo's voice was cool and detached. A reminder that he was here for her, not himself.

As she thought it he lifted his arm off her waist and rolled away. Ally stifled the cry of dismay that rose to her lips.

'Thank you, Angelo.' She pulled the bedding tight around herself and turned to him, but he was already getting up from the bed. 'That was kind of you.'

That halted him in his tracks. 'Kind?' He paused, a wry expression on his face. 'It was the least I could do after...'

He shook his head and her mood tumbled. It

couldn't be clearer that he felt uncomfortable about having sex with her. That he didn't want a repeat.

Ally wrapped her fragile defences around herself and pasted on a smile that hopefully looked more real than it felt. 'Of course. But, again, thank you.'

This time his gaze held hers and a frisson of connection crackled through her. Was she the only one to feel it?

'Rest now. I'll have Rosetta bring you breakfast.'

Under veiling eyelashes she watched him pull on his clothes, his movements quick, almost urgent. Because he had business elsewhere or because he didn't want to be around her any longer? Maybe he feared she'd read too much into the sex they'd shared. Still, she couldn't stop the question. 'And what are you going to do?'

'Start the search for your identity. With luck, and my resources, it won't take too long to find out who you are and where you came from.'

'Wonderful.' She pinned on a smile that felt too tight across her cheeks. 'Thank you.'

It would be a relief finally to know who she was, so she could resume her real life. Yet why did she feel desolate at the prospect of leaving the villa? No, not the villa. Leaving Angelo Ricci.

Realisation sheared through her like a dropping blade.

Angelo said he despised Alexa but hatred was close to love. He still felt incredibly strongly about his ex-wife and that was what Ally had tapped into.

But had she done more? Had she done something silly, like fall for a man who saw her only as a pale imitation of the woman he'd once cared for?

Suddenly Ally was terrified that was exactly what she'd done.

CHAPTER TWELVE

ALLY HAD SPENT a week with the man she'd believed to be her ex-husband. Now, three days into her second week with Angelo Ricci, everything had changed.

Angelo was the perfect host, ensuring she was comfortable while he pursued his quest to uncover her identity.

He was considerate and supportive. Yet Ally longed for more. A spark of the emotion they'd shared. Of the passion that still twisted, like a slow-burning flame, deep within her. Even a flicker of anger would do if she couldn't have his desire. Anything to indicate he felt *something* for her.

She told herself she shouldn't crave his touch. But that made no difference. No matter how hard she tried she couldn't forget that magical interlude when he'd shown her a whole new world. With him she'd come alive in ways she hadn't thought possible. As if sex were more than a physical experience.

But Angelo didn't share her feelings. He was friendly and considerate but that was all.

No more burning glances. No more sizzling passion.

Because you're not the woman he really wanted. He thought you were Alexa.

Ally shivered. The speed with which Angelo had left her bed that morning had confirmed it. He'd spent the night with her out of pity and guilt. Ally had read that in his eyes, and in the shadows that darkened his features when he thought she wasn't watching. He felt sorry for her and blamed himself for what had happened between them.

As if she hadn't been a more than willing participant!

Ally tried to tell herself she'd been carried away by anger that night. But she'd wanted Angelo from the first. She'd been attracted even when he was furious and dismissive, and when he'd been nice...he'd undone her utterly.

She pulled her borrowed gardening gloves higher up her hands and frowned at the arching rose bush before her. Instead of blush pink blooms she saw dark eyes and a haunted, handsome face in her mind's eye.

Angelo was doing everything he could to track down her name and her past. He must be paying a fortune for the investigators but he was determined to get answers for her.

Because he wants you gone as soon as possible.

She drew herself up, searching for the strength she needed. Was it any surprise she felt as if she was living a half-life? Maybe her anguished feelings weren't just because of Angelo. It made sense she was unsettled from not knowing who she was.

Surely it was impossible to fall for a man she'd known a bare week.

If she kept telling herself that…

'Ally?'

Adrenaline shot through her at the sound of his voice. She spun around and felt that familiar dazzle of excitement as their eyes met. How could a man grow more scrumptious by the day?

'Hi Angelo.' Did she sound breathless? Her pulse was pounding so fast she couldn't tell.

'Enzo's trusted you alone with the roses?' He nodded to the secateurs in her gloved hands. 'He must really respect your gardening skills. He watches my mother like a hawk when she wants to get involved here.'

Ally shrugged. Angelo made too much out of something simple. Was he trying too hard to sound casual? But, taking in his relaxed features, she dismissed the notion. *She* was the one pining for things she couldn't have.

'I'm just deadheading. Nothing major.'

'Even so, it's no small thing, winning his trust, believe me.'

Angelo paused and her pulse thudded. 'Do you have news? Have you found out anything?'

She had recurring nightmares about never recovering her past, living the rest of her life in this strange limbo. It would be fantastic finally to get a lead on who she was. Yet at the same time she felt butterflies inside at the idea of leaving and never seeing Angelo again.

'I'm afraid not.' He frowned. 'But we *are* making progress. Eventually I'll have good news for you.'

He smiled reassuringly and Ally felt that familiar warmth inside her chest. She knew that, as well as trying to trace her movements in Italy, Angelo had hired people to locate Alexa, figuring there must be a familial link between her and Ally. Surely soon there would be a breakthrough.

'I came to see if you felt like an outing. It's a glorious day and I thought an excursion might be welcome. You've been here nine days and the only place you've been is next door.'

Ally fought to keep her voice calm, while inside she felt like dancing a jig. An outing with Angelo, just for fun and not because he thought it was his duty. 'What did you have in mind?'

His cheeks creased as he smiled down at her, as if reading her pleasure. 'Capri. It's calm enough to see the Blue Grotto. Then we could eat at a restaurant I know with the best views in southern Italy.'

'I'd love it!'

'More salad?'

Angelo held out the bowl so Ally could help herself. He liked her enthusiasm for good food, sampling each dish slowly, identifying the flavours, before tucking in wholeheartedly.

They had a secluded spot on the restaurant terrace and inevitably his attention was riveted to this fascinating woman rather than the glorious view.

'My mother would like you,' he said, surprising himself.

Ally stopped with a piece of fish poised on her fork. 'She would? How so?'

'She's a fine cook, she'd like the way you appreciate what you eat.'

Angelo watched Ally pop the morsel into her mouth and chew. He tried not to stare at those full pink lips and reached for his wine, gulping down a mouthful and ignoring the tightening of his jeans. In that pretty sundress and wearing a wide-brimmed sunhat purchased at a shop by the port, Ally looked fresh and alluring.

It had been two days since they'd made love and there hadn't been an hour of that time when he hadn't imagined or dreamed about doing it again.

Angelo reached again for his glass then put it down. He needed to keep a clear head around her.

He guessed Ally didn't realise how seductive she looked or how enticing her smiles. Unlike Alexa, her warmth was real and natural. She'd dazzled the young boatman who took them into the Blue Grotto so much that Angelo had wondered if the guy would follow them ashore and become a nuisance.

'I'd never dream of wasting food, especially when it tastes like this. I know how much effort goes into cooking a great meal. Even something simple, like a good, old-fashioned apple pie, takes time and know-how to get the pastry just right.'

Angelo caught the significance of Ally's words though it appeared she didn't. She was a cook as well as a gardener?

'Besides, it would be criminal not to make the most of this place.' Her gesture encompassed the terrace, perched high with a view over the town below and the sea that changed colour as the sun moved. 'Thank you for bringing me here, Angelo. It's brilliant!'

No, it was her smile that was brilliant. And her enthusiasm. She'd been enthralled by everything, her questions about the sights they visited revealing a questioning mind and a readiness to be pleased.

'It's absolutely my pleasure, Ally. I'm enjoying myself too.'

How long since he'd made the effort to play tourist with someone? Or enjoyed it so much?

He truly had become a workaholic as his sister claimed. He attended black tie events for charity or business but couldn't recall his last meal out simply for pleasure. Maybe too he'd grown selfish since Alexa, rarely exerting himself for anyone except his family.

'There's something I need to tell you, Ally.' She looked up questioningly. 'I apologised for my behaviour when I thought you were Alexa but you deserve an explanation.'

Sharing intimate details of his life didn't come naturally but he couldn't ignore the urge to explain to Ally. Not to excuse his actions but because she deserved to understand.

'Go on.'

Looking into her bright gaze, this didn't feel nearly the chore it had seemed before. There was no judgement there, only encouragement. She was a remarkable woman.

'I never explained why Alexa's betrayal cut so deep.'

'You're a powerful, successful man, used to making major corporate decisions. Finding you'd been tricked would undermine your confidence in your judgement.'

Angelo's eyes widened. 'I'm so transparent?'

She shrugged. Was that a flicker of amusement? 'Hardly. At first I found you almost impossible to read.'

'And now?'

His heart thundered as he met that stunning lilac gaze. For the first time he found himself drawn by the idea of someone, *this woman*, having his measure, understanding him. In the past he'd cultivated an air of impenetrability, a valuable tool as he grappled with corporate challenges.

But life wasn't all about work. Increasingly he'd begun to think about finding more satisfaction in his private life. To actually *have* a private life, rather than casual flings and too-brief breaks from work.

Colour caressed Ally's cheekbones. 'Now I see the caring, decent man behind the powerbroker.'

Did she? It felt as if he'd done too little for her.

'Alexa *did* hurt my pride and made me question my judgement. But her real sin was hurting my family.' He twisted the stem of his wineglass. 'Our family was close and when my father died we were devastated. My mother in particular. She fell apart.' He paused, remembering how her breakdown had made him vow never to be so vulnerable, even as he'd understood her pain. 'I tried to fill the gap, taking care of her and my younger sister. I'd have done it anyway, but it was the last thing I promised my father.'

'That's a big responsibility.'

'So was stepping into his shoes as CEO. All the pundits said I was too young. They waited for me to fail. But I refused to let my father down. It was a rocky road but I eventually proved myself.'

He'd worked ridiculous hours, barely taking breaks.

'But still I worried about my mother. She'd lost her joy in life. It was only when Alexa declared she was pregnant that I saw the old spark in Mamma's eyes.'

'Ah.'

Angelo nodded. Ally had guessed what came next. 'My mother and sister were thrilled at me settling down and at the prospect of a baby. It began to feel like the old days, until the truth came out. That crushed my mother, not just that there was no baby but that the woman I'd married was so awful. I had to watch her slide back into depression.' He paused, his gut cramping. 'My sister was damaged by it too. Ever since then she's avoided relationships, worrying the only reason a man would pursue her is for her money. It's destroyed her confidence and ability to trust.'

'Oh, Angelo, I'm so sorry.'

'They're doing better now.' His mamma was, at least. 'But I blame myself for the hurt I brought them.'

'It wasn't your fault!'

'I was the one who brought Alexa into our lives and let them believe in our marriage. They thought our family was healing with a new generation. That's why I reacted so badly to you. Why I refused to give you the benefit of the doubt. Seeing you dredged up all that pain and reminded me of how I'd failed them.'

Warm fingers closed on his hand. 'I'm sure they'd disagree.' Angelo met her eyes and was surprised to see her look stern. 'You take too much on yourself.'

He shook his head. 'I promised to protect them.'

'You care about them very much, don't you?'

'Of course. More than anything. They're family.'

Something flared in her eyes then disappeared.

'It was Alexa who lied, not you. What about the damage she did to you?'

Angelo withdrew his hand. Not because he disliked Ally's touch but because it made him feel too much. Made him want too much.

'I just wanted you to understand. You deserved an explanation.'

Ally regarded him silently and for the first time in for ever it felt as if someone saw past his persona of power and competence to the fault lines deep within.

'Thank you. I do feel better, understanding a little.' She paused. 'Tell me about them. You said your mother is a good cook. What's her speciality?'

Gratitude filled him at Ally's understanding and acceptance. At her change of subject, as if she knew how hard it was to speak of this.

'Seafood.' He forced himself to smile, though he felt wound too tight. 'Her family is from Venice so that's a speciality. But my sister developed a seafood allergy, so Mamma has branched out a lot. Her beef *ragù* has to be tasted to be believed, and her desserts…!'

Ally chuckled, the sound like liquid sunshine, bright as she leaned close, her face alight. Angelo felt his rigid muscles relax.

'You have a sweet tooth? What's her special-ity? Tiramisu? Zabaglione?'

He was about to say she knew a lot about Ital-ian cuisine but stopped himself. If Ally became self-conscious about the information she revealed it might stop.

'She makes those, but her lemon cake is my favourite.'

'Really? I have the best recipe for a citron tart. It has a luscious lemon filling, topped with slices of lemon sprinkled with icing sugar that you car-amelise under a flame. My gran taught me to make it. It's her favourite.'

Ally's words stopped with an abrupt snap of teeth. Slowly she lowered her knife and fork to the table. Her gaze sought his, a hazy lavender stare that now looked lost.

'I did it again, didn't I?' She gulped a shaky breath. 'I can remember tiny things. I can even, almost, picture the kitchen where I learned to cook, but nothing else. Not even her face. Just her silver hair and the warmth of her voice.'

Ally sounded so forlorn, her eyes huge with emotion, that Angelo didn't think twice, just took her hand in both of his. This generous woman needed support.

'It's a good sign that you're starting to remem-ber snippets.'

'But why *little* things? Why not my name or address? Or who my family is?'

Her voice rose to a wobbly note that pierced him. She'd been so brave and positive. It was too easy to forget how frightening her memory loss must be because of her determined good humour. Yet knowing what she'd endured because of him cut a sweeping gash through his belly.

'It's little things now but soon it'll be bigger things. Just be patient and it will all work out.'

Angelo had no idea if that were true but he willed it to be so.

He couldn't recall wishing for anything so hard. Not since his father had died, leaving Angelo alternately wishing for more time with his beloved *papà*, and to be the man he had to be for his family's sake.

'You'll see, Ally. Stay positive and it'll all eventually come back to you.'

'But what if it's something awful? Something I'd rather not face?'

He squeezed her hand, wishing he could take her in his arms and hold her, comfort her with an embrace. His arms ached with the effort of holding back. 'Whatever happened, you won't be alone, Ally. I'll be with you. I promise. You'll be safe.'

Angelo leaned in, close enough to inhale her

delicate scent. Close enough to kiss those trembling lips.

But he didn't, despite the almost overwhelming urge to do so. Because it wasn't simple reassurance he longed to give her.

He wanted to kiss Ally for *himself*. To satisfy his own greedy longing for her.

One night with her was nowhere near enough. He wanted so much more. But he had no right. She needed his support, not his lust, no matter how fantastic they'd been together. He had an obligation to care for her.

Maybe, one day, when she'd regained her memory of the past... But he couldn't allow himself to fantasise about that now.

'Thank you, Angelo. It makes a huge difference to know I'm not totally alone.' Ally's eyes shone and her mouth pulled up in a crooked smile that tugged at his heartstrings. 'You're very kind.'

Angelo almost snorted in self-disgust. Kind? Kind would have been giving her the benefit of the doubt earlier.

'Now you're exaggerating. I was an ogre in those early days. But keep saying it, Ally. I like hearing it.'

Far too much.

As expected, his words drew a genuine smile. Angelo liked her ready sense of humour. 'Well, you're a lot easier to handle now than you were a week ago.'

'That's something, at least.' Angelo tried and almost succeeded in not thinking about Ally handling him in the way he wanted, naked flesh to naked flesh. Maybe that was what made him blurt out, 'I have an idea. Something that might trigger your memory.'

As soon as he said it, and saw excitement brighten her features, he wondered if he'd been wise to mention it. Because there was a risk involved, a risk to Ally, and she'd already been through enough. That was why he hadn't spoken of it sooner. But it was too late.

'Tell me!' Her hand turned in his as she gripped his fingers. What did you have in mind?'

'You were walking in Oliver's garden when you started to remember something so strongly that you felt ill. Maybe there was something there that triggered your memory. Something about the place maybe?'

Her brow furrowed in concentration. 'Maybe there *was* something...' She paused. 'Some smell. Maybe from a plant? Or am I imagining that?'

Angelo nodded. 'Perhaps, if nothing else comes to mind in the next few days, we could visit Oliver and retrace your steps. See if anything happens.' He wasn't sure it was the best idea, given how it had affected her last time, but Ally was getting upset and he hated to see her distraught.

'Why didn't I think of that? It's brilliant.' She smiled up at him and it felt like a burst of sunlight exploding inside. 'Thank you, Angelo!'

It was late when they returned to the villa. The violet dusk had fallen, settling like a dark blanket on the island. Ally revelled in the warm evening air. It felt like a caress on her bare arms as they entered Angelo's home, the scents from the garden creating a heady perfume.

Angelo's original plan for a couple of hours on Capri had turned into a full day excursion to see the sights, ending with them sharing dinner at a restaurant which had been both spectacular and charming.

Ally had loved every minute. Seeing new things. Mingling with other people. The beauty of the island. But especially the ease between her and Angelo. The barrier between them had dropped and she didn't feel so obviously that he held back from her. Though it was clear he wasn't about to sweep her into his arms like she wanted.

But they'd spent the day as friends, which Ally treasured. It wasn't as good as being lovers, yet Angelo made her feel special.

'Thanks for a wonderful day, Angelo. I had the

best time.' Her pulse quickened as she met his dark eyes. Would she ever get over him? The answer had to be *yes*. She had to find out who she was, the sooner the better. 'Do you think Oliver is home?'

Angelo's frown told her he wasn't eager to go there, which was odd, as it had been his idea.

'It's easy enough to find out.' He took his phone from his pocket just as it rang. His expression as he glanced at the screen told her the incoming call was important. 'I'll answer this first. It won't take long.'

Ally nodded and headed for the stairs. She might as well put away the sunhat Angelo had bought her.

But once in her room she couldn't settle. Her thoughts kept turning to Angelo.

He'd opened himself to her in a way she'd never expected. Understanding his self-blame over the impact of Alexa's behaviour and how it had coloured his attitude when she'd washed up on his beach made her feel better. She was drawn by his protectiveness to his family, despite believing he laid too heavy a burden on himself.

He was a complex, thoughtful, surprising man.

His apology and his promise to be there for her if she needed him had broken through the brittle casing of fear around her heart. That made her feel stronger and ready to face her past, even if at the same time she realised how vulnerable she was to him.

With Angelo at her side she felt she could face almost anything. But soon they'd have to go their separate ways.

Regret was a sour tang, filling her mouth. Yet at the same time impatience grew. He wasn't interested in her. She wasn't one of the chosen few who truly mattered to him. His tender expression when he'd spoken of his family had made her almost jealous of them! How selfish was that?

The longer she stayed here, the harder it would be to hide her feelings. She was living in his home, seeing him every day. Even the clothes she wore had been bought by him. Was it any wonder she felt tied to him?

As Ally paced the lamplight caught the sparkle of purple and blue on her feet. The gorgeous strappy sandals that Angelo had bought her on Capri. They were pretty and jewelled and Ally knew instinctively they were the sort of expensive treat she would never have bought for herself.

She loved them.

She swallowed hard, her throat aching as an upswell of emotion caught her.

It wasn't just the sandals she loved. It was Angelo.

Ally had tried not to think about it but hiding from such a blatant truth didn't work.

Nor did telling herself it was impossible to feel so much after such a short time.

Falling for a man who was emotionally attached to his ex-wife was asking for trouble. It could go nowhere. Because, despite the damage she'd caused, Alexa was still important, still at the centre of his thoughts. He'd made love to Ally, believing she was Alexa.

She *had* to get back her memory and leave. Go somewhere where she could try to get over him.

Ally hurried from the room, her skin prickling with urgency as if ants crawled over her.

When she got downstairs she heard the murmur of Angelo's voice from the study. He'd only been on the phone a few minutes but she couldn't wait. Besides, she didn't want to face him now. She'd rather do this on her own.

Soon after, Oliver's housekeeper led her onto his terrace and turned on the outdoor lights. Signor Branston was tied up on a video call but of course she could wait in the garden until he was free.

Ally resisted the impulse to break into a run as the housekeeper left. Instead she took her time, trying to breathe slowly as she approached the enclosed garden where she'd walked with Oliver.

She paused at the entrance, her palm on the column of a jasmine-covered pergola. The scent filled the evening air but it wasn't the perfume that had sparked her memory.

Fighting anticipation and nerves, she stepped onto the path and approached the sundial at the centre of the space.

Still nothing. Maybe Angelo was wrong. Maybe it was the conversation with Oliver that had brought back her past. Perhaps...

Ally slammed to a halt as a heavy waft of perfume engulfed her. Her nostrils twitched and something feathered the back of her neck, the dance of phantom fingers across tightening skin. Slowly she inhaled, drawing the pungent aroma deep into her lungs. It was familiar.

Looking down, she saw blue-grey foliage and purple spears of flowers.

Lavender.

On the word came a jumbled rush of memory. Sights. Voices. Faces. Laughter. The warmth of home.

Relief filled Ally and she smiled, the fear she'd held in so tight finally lifting.

There was Uncle Ben on a tractor, his tatty hat shading his face. Long rows of lavender, dark purple and pungent in the midday sun. White blossoms in the orchard, birds singing in the branches. Cobwebs glistening with jewels of dew in the dawn light. The comforting cluck of chickens as they pecked their way through the garden. The smell of wood smoke curling from the old chimney on a winter's morning and the cuddly warmth of a hand-knitted jumper protecting her from the cold as she stepped onto frost-stiffened grass.

Wonderful as they were, the bombardment of recollections rocked her and Ally made for a stone bench. Her fingers closed tight around it as she sank, anchoring herself as she grew light-headed.

She closed her eyes, hearing rain drumming on the iron roof of the old farmhouse. The chirrup of frogs in the dam. Belle's eager bark, telling her to hurry. The sound of humming, an old lullaby she'd known all her life.

Abruptly the relief and lightness vanished.

Joy was eclipsed in a devastating rush of desolation that froze everything inside her.

Ally heard herself gasp. A sliver of ice pierced her chest as fragmented recollections shifted and pieced together.

Then the tears started to slide down her face.

CHAPTER THIRTEEN

ANGELO FOUND HER in a secluded part of the garden. Near where he'd seen her with Oliver.

She sat with her back to him but even in the muted light he knew something was wrong. Her shoulders were hunched and her head hung low. Fear punched the air from his lungs.

He hurried forward, silently cursing. His sister had had a small crisis days ago so he'd felt compelled to take her call. It had been good to hear her bright and confident, having dealt with her problem, but he regretted those ten minutes on the phone.

Today with Ally had been special. He'd revelled in her delight and the sparkle in her eyes when she looked at him. He'd basked in her approval at his idea to jog her memory but he should have kept quiet, respecting his sixth sense that it could be devastating for her.

'Ally.'

He sank down beside her, registering the tight pull of her lips and the rigid set of her jaw. Something dropped from her chin and he realised she was weeping.

His chest turned over. It reminded him of the roiling pain he'd felt when his father died.

Seeing Ally lost to grief undid him. He felt helpless though he wanted so much to make things better.

He covered one cold, trembling hand with his. 'I'm here, *cara*. You're not alone.'

Angelo moved closer, wrapping his arm around her, feeling her shudder as she drew in each breath. She felt fragile. Her feistiness and determination had been swamped by something. Bad news, he guessed.

He should have been here with her, not left her to face this alone. He should have guessed she'd be impatient to know, deciding not to wait for him.

'Whatever it is, Ally, we'll face it together.'

She took a shuddering breath and lifted her head. The sight of her pale features, drawn with pain, made him ache.

Angelo lifted her hand and pressed his mouth to it. It was a heartfelt kiss, not of physical passion but of something stronger and deeper. He wanted to give her his strength and help her through this crisis.

Her lips curved in a sad parody of a smile that cracked his heart. 'I'm okay, Angelo, just coming to terms with the past.' She paused. 'The good news is I'm not dying of some terrible illness. I'll be fine. I just need time to adjust.'

Angelo didn't release her. 'What can I do? Do you need to be somewhere? Do you want me to make arrangements?'

Ally shook her head. 'There's nothing. Thank you.'

Angelo said nothing, wanting to give her time and space. Whatever had caused this grief, it was her choice whether to share it with him. He wouldn't intrude.

Ally was grateful for Angelo's presence. It calmed her, made her realise she could face this. When he'd kissed her hand it had felt as if he shared something vital with her. Something that made this marginally easier.

How different he was from the man she'd first met.

She could imagine herself building a future with this Angelo, a man who could be gentle as well as strong. But it wasn't possible. Whatever he felt for her was mixed up with his attraction to his ex.

Ally sat straighter and wiped the tears from her face with her free hand. Angelo didn't move his arm from around her shoulders. For that she was grateful. It felt better to be held.

Still he didn't question her. She looked into his eyes, black in this light, and her heart swelled with tenderness. He could be understanding as well as demanding.

'My name's Alison Dennehy, but I've always been called Ally.' Her whispered words to Angelo on the beach that first day had been right. 'I come from Tasmania, the island state at the south of Australia.'

Angelo nodded his encouragement but didn't press for more. He was letting her take her time and the realisation made something shift hard inside her.

'It was the lavender.' She pointed to the clump growing near the sundial. 'I brushed it and the smell brought it all back.' She smiled and felt her facial muscles pull high on one side. Maybe it was more of a grimace. 'I grew up on a lavender farm and apple orchard.'

'No wonder the perfume sparked memories.'

Ally nodded. 'It's a potent scent and they say there's nothing like smell to evoke the past.'

That was something which had particularly interested her in her work with essences.

So much was coming back. There were blanks still but she had enough sense of herself and her past to understand what had happened. She rubbed her hand up her bare arm as a glacial shiver prickled her skin.

'Your family is still on the farm?'

'Yes,' she said quickly, feeling pain stab. 'My uncle lives in the old farmhouse now with his wife and children.' Ally swallowed hard. 'I lived there from the age of four. After my parents died in a car crash my gran raised me.' Angelo squeezed her hand and she was grateful for his understanding. 'The pair of us lived together there for years.'

'Just the two of you?'

His voice told her he'd guessed what was coming. She inclined her head. 'Just Gran and me. Uncle Ben worked on the farm but lived in town.'

'And you liked it there.'

It wasn't a question. Ally wondered what Angelo heard in her voice.

'I adored it. No wonder I like helping Enzo in the garden.' She forced a laugh. 'It's where I'm most at home. Growing things, keeping bees, making things from what we grew, like herbal essences, soaps and scents.' She met Angelo's gaze. 'I'm good at it too. I'd developed a range of lavender and honey products.'

She'd planned to make that her future.

'I'm sure you are. You seem a natural.'

Ally looked at their linked hands, knowing she

should withdraw from him but not having the strength.

'I'm not a city girl like Alexa.'

She felt him start. 'So you *are* related?'

'We're cousins. Our mothers were identical twins. That's why we look similar, but she's a few years older.'

And in experience even older. Poor Alexa. Despite what Angelo had revealed, Ally knew there were reasons for her cousin's behaviour, if not excuses, starting with an abusive stepfather who'd skewed her ideas about relationships.

'You've seen her recently?'

'Not for years. She visited Gran and stayed for a while. That's how I knew about this place. She spoke about the island with such affection, said it was the most beautiful, peaceful place in the world. I always thought that if I had the chance I'd visit.'

She paused, remembering why she now had time for travel. 'I think she must have visited soon after your divorce. She was troubled and Gran has always been good at listening to problems in a way that helps you work out what to do about them.'

Ally swallowed that hot ache in her throat. 'Alexa was at some sort of crossroads.' She flashed him a look. Her impression was that

Alexa didn't like the woman she'd become. 'She's living interstate now, working for an organisation that supports victims of sexual violence.'

Angelo's eyebrows lifted in surprise. 'She sounds like a different woman to the one I knew.'

'Perhaps she is.'

Ally waited for him to pump her for more information about the woman who'd figured so large in his life. The woman he still desired.

His next words surprised her, for they weren't about Alexa.

'You remember something else, don't you, Ally?' His voice was coaxing and gentle tears prickled the back of her eyes again. 'Your grandmother?'

She inclined her head. Of course it was Gran. Every memory she'd had until now had been linked to her.

'She died.' Ally's voice was harsh, the words sticking to her tongue so she had to force them out. Her chest ached as she drew air into tight lungs. 'She was driving the tractor while I was out. They say she had a heart attack at the wheel and died instantly, probably before the tractor overturned on an embankment.'

'Ah, *tesoro*.' Angelo gathered her close and somehow she was sitting on his lap, her head tucked beneath his chin. The warmth of his big frame and the steady beat of his heart against her ear were reassuring in a world suddenly fluid with broken images and shocking hurt.

Another painful breath, another painful memory. 'I came home and found her and Belle lying there.'

Her words ran out. The memory was too vivid.

'Belle?' Angelo's voice was sharp.

'Our old border collie. We'd had her since I was young. She was devoted to me and Gran.' Ally bit her bottom lip, willing it not to wobble, though the anguish had reached an unbearable level.

'A double tragedy, then. When Rocco, my childhood dog, died it almost broke my heart.'

Ally nodded, suppressing a snuffle. She could picture Angelo with a dog. He had a kind heart, she'd discovered. She could imagine him loyal and loving.

'It seems silly, but losing them both together made it more devastating.'

Especially as she'd been confronted with the sight of them both— She sucked in a sharp breath and forced her thoughts elsewhere.

Ally barely had any memories of her parents. It was Gran who'd looked after her when she was sick, listened to her dreams, encouraging her and laughing with her. As for Belle, Ally remembered her as a puppy, her raspy tongue licking, and as an older dog, slowed by arthritis but still faithful and loving. Still insisting on riding the tractor though she needed help to get up.

'It's not silly at all. It makes perfect sense.' He paused. 'No wonder you took a holiday to get away for a while.'

'It's not quite like that.'

Ally straightened in his embrace and immediately his arm slid away, releasing her and giving her the chance to move away if she wished. She didn't wish. She wanted to stay in Angelo's arms for ever, but it was enough to remind her it was time to look after herself, not turn to him for comfort.

She forced herself to rise, swaying a little before finding her balance. She sensed him stand behind her, felt his body heat.

'What is it, Ally? There's more, isn't there?'

It was as if he read her emotions, despite her determination to control them.

Ally gave a strained shrug. 'I had to leave the farm. Gran and Uncle Ben were joint owners and when Gran died...' She took a deep breath, staring across the beautifully manicured garden. 'Uncle Ben lost money on a separate business deal, an investment gone wrong. He's badly in debt and his family lost their home. They needed somewhere to live.'

Angelo's voice was hard. 'So they moved onto the farm and forced you out while you were grieving?'

'They didn't *force* me. It made sense to move out.'

Besides, it wouldn't be the same living there without Gran.

'Don't you have a share in the property? Especially if you were helping to run the farm?'

Angelo stepped in front of her, his face sombre, and she saw the businessman in his expression, looking for leverage on her behalf.

Warmth trickled through her cold body at his earnest look. He really was concerned about her. She reckoned he'd be an indomitable ally should she need one.

But the sad truth was that the sooner she got away from his orbit the better for her peace of mind. He tied her in knots and made her long for what could never be.

'I inherited a minority share of the farm. But Uncle Ben can't afford to buy me out at the moment and I'm not pressing him for the money.' She forced a smile to stiff lips. 'As for sharing a small farmhouse with my aunt, uncle and four rambunctious boys under ten, that's not an option.'

Angelo didn't smile back. His brows contracted in a scowl.

'Look, Uncle Ben isn't trying to cheat me. He'll buy me out when things turn around. Meanwhile Gran left me a bit of cash. That's what I used to travel here. I'm on my way to the south of France, to visit the lavender fields and the perfumeries. But I wanted to see this place that Alexa raved about. That's why I flew to Rome first.'

Angelo nodded. 'A holiday. An excellent idea after all that's happened.'

Ally spread her hands. 'Originally it was going to be more than a holiday.' That was in the days before Gran's death when she'd dreamed of a fact-finding trip. 'I've always been interested in scent-making. I'd planned to use the lavender farm as a springboard into that.'

She stopped. Without the farm, she needed to find a new dream. Uncle Ben had plans for the place that didn't include perfume-making or bee-keeping. When she returned to Australia she'd have to find a new job and a new home. A different dream.

'But, yes, it's a short vacation. A once-in-a-life-time opportunity to see something of the world.'

Because she'd had to get away and it was easier to head for the place she'd always wanted to visit than devise a new itinerary.

Ally didn't have formal qualifications. When she did find work it would probably be poorly paid. She doubted she'd have another chance for overseas travel.

She looked from the garden to the tall man watching her, the man she cared for too much, and told herself it was a good thing she was moving on.

Angelo was protective but that was all. His first thought, on learning she remembered her past, was to ask where she wanted to be and if he could help her get there.

He didn't want her as she did him. He merely felt sorry for her and obliged to help her. Even the sexual attraction between them had been short-lived, a mistake on his part because he'd believed her to be someone else.

Ally felt her heart crumple as the last of her dreams shrivelled. She angled her chin up and turned away. 'Shall we go? I'd rather not see Oliver tonight.'

Angelo poured a glass of red wine with numb fingers. His muscles were taut, his movements uncoordinated, because witnessing Ally in distress had undone him.

He knew about grief, but he still had his beloved mother and sister. Who did Ally have?

'Here. It will warm you up.'

She looked up from the settee where she'd collapsed on their return. For a moment he thought she'd refuse, as she'd refused all alcohol before. Instead she reached for the glass, carefully grasping it so that their hands didn't brush, before taking a cautious sip.

Regret pierced him. A yearning for her touch. The profound need to *connect*. She was hurting and he wanted to hold her, comfort her.

It would comfort him too, having her in his arms. Because he'd missed her there, though they'd only had one night together.

He swung away and poured himself a glass of wine, despising his neediness. This wasn't about him but what was best for Ally.

It seemed that, despite her readiness to sink into his embrace half an hour ago, she didn't want solace from him now. Would that change if he gave her time and space?

An unseen weight pressed between his shoulder blades.

'What can I do, Ally? What would help?'

If he could be useful he'd feel better. He was accustomed to taking charge and making things happen.

Shadowed eyes met his. They looked dazed and his fingers curled tighter around the stem of his glass.

'You offered to arrange transport.'

Angelo's heart shrank. 'Of course. When you've had time to sort yourself out—'

She shook her head, her honey-coloured hair sliding around her neck. 'There's no point in delaying.'

Her gaze shifted to the ruby wine in her glass.

Because she couldn't bear to look at him? He stiffened.

Angelo had imagined today that they'd reached a new level of understanding, friendship even. But tonight's revelations made it starkly clear how poorly he'd treated her, a woman grieving the loss of a loved one and, if he read the situation right, her dreams too.

'I'd like you to stay. Take your time and recover completely. I'll look after you—'

'No!' Her strident syllable gashed his windpipe, stopping his words. 'I don't need you to look after me! I'm not your responsibility. What I *need* is to leave.'

Angelo heard the hard, cold truth in her voice. The distress. He shouldn't be surprised that she wanted to escape from here, from him, as soon as she could.

It was a mistake, letting her go. He felt it in every atom of his body. But he remembered his sister telling him he was overprotective, remembered Ally concurring, saying he'd gone too far in shouldering responsibility for Alexa's actions. Protective instinct and selfish need battled against the desperation he read in Ally's face. Her need for freedom, away from him.

'If that's what you want...' It nearly killed him to say it.

'It's time I got on with my real life.'

A life that didn't include him. It was a hammer blow.

Once he'd wished this woman elsewhere. Now he didn't want her to go. Not only because he felt protective but because he wanted...more.

That was a first. He was an expert at ending relationships with women but had no experience maintaining them. He hadn't had the guts to seek a meaningful long-term relationship because he'd feared that caring led to too much pain.

Yet suddenly that was exactly what he wanted, to be with Ally long-term.

Everything about her called to him. Not just her looks, but her stubborn strength, her determination to make the best of her difficult situation. Her stoicism as she'd weathered one blow after another. Her charm, humour and the friendly way she had with everyone, from the movie mogul next door to the gardener and various strangers.

She was thoughtful yet engaging. She was sexy

in a way that made every atom in his body sit up and beg for another taste of her body.

She was exactly what he'd never realised he wanted.

He, who'd never permitted himself to imagine feeling so much for any woman.

The knowledge didn't strike like a blow. Instead it infused his blood, spreading through every vein, artery and capillary until it was a glow warming his body from the inside. Angelo had never experienced anything like it.

But it was *not* what Ally needed to hear tonight. She had enough to deal with.

After what had passed between them he *had* to give her freedom to make this choice without interference. He owed her that much.

Reluctantly he spoke. 'I'll make some calls—'

'Thank you. I'll leave tomorrow.' Angelo's pulse skipped. So soon? 'I need transport to Naples. I stayed at a *pensione* there and left my luggage in storage while I came down to the coast for the day.'

Ally waited for him to nod and agree but the words wouldn't come.

A primitive part of him wanted to do whatever it took to keep her here.

Angelo exhaled slowly. He could never do that. Ally's independence was crucial, especially after she'd been cooped up here so long, hemmed in by memory loss.

'I'll call the doctor. He'd better check you over first. When he gives the all-clear, I'll organise transport.'

Angelo paused, mind racing, searching for an excuse to delay because, no matter how much she wanted to leave, it didn't *feel* right. Yet how could he impose his will on her? The way she'd flinched from him, stridently rejecting his suggestion she stay, was too revealing.

'Give me your contact details, in case you run into trouble.' A new thought struck. 'Or if there are consequences from the other night. Condoms can fail.'

The idea of a child evoked powerful emotion but it wasn't the trapped feeling he'd experienced when Alexa had told him she was pregnant.

Ally's face jerked up, such dismay on her features that his nebulous imaginings disintegrated along with his pride.

That look said everything. Ally might resemble her cousin physically but the thought of being tied to him, even with his fortune and social standing, clearly held no allure.

His conscience told him he'd got his just deserts. She'd made her preference clear. Her first thought was to get away from him as soon as possible.

He wanted to rage and protest. To stop her leaving.

But Angelo Ricci was a civilised man who respected a woman's wishes. He swallowed his wine in one gulp, put down his glass and wished Ally goodnight, amazed he could still speak given the almighty ache opening up inside him.

Then he strode from the room before he did something utterly selfish, like ask her to stay, for *his* sake.

CHAPTER FOURTEEN

ALLY HUNG UP her damp towel in the tiny hotel bathroom and wrapped a cotton robe around herself.

Tonight was her last night in Provence. She'd spent a week exploring the countryside, the quaint stone-built villages, seeing the fields of lavender and other flowers and visiting a perfume factory.

It had been exciting, memorable and poignant. Because it made her think of her beloved gran and the plans Ally had had for the future.

When she returned to Australia her life would change. She'd have to look for work in the city. Uncle Ben couldn't afford to employ her. He planned to run the farm alone with his wife till their finances were better. Ally didn't want to live nearby, hankering for what she couldn't have.

She shook her head and grabbed a comb, pulling it through her hair. It was the story of her life right now, clearing out of places because she couldn't bear to be close to what she couldn't have.

Angelo.

The name feathered into her brain like a waft of beckoning lavender-scented breeze from the surrounding fields.

She'd left him nine days ago and the yearning hadn't subsided. Would it ever? She'd so wanted to stay with him, until he spoke of looking after her, as if she were yet another responsibility he'd taken on. A duty. Not because he couldn't bear to be without her.

'You have to give it time,' she told herself.

No more thinking of Angelo, who'd left her in Naples with such a severe, brooding expression that she guessed some problem had arisen at his bank. She'd cut short their goodbyes, not trusting her emotions, giving him a quick handshake and running into the *pensione* where she'd stored her luggage before he could say anything.

Of course, that hadn't been the end of it. He'd been on her mind every hour since.

She'd imagined she saw his gleaming dark sports car as she'd made her way through the thronged Naples streets. Her spirits had soared at the railway station when she thought she saw him, head and shoulders above the crowd, as if he'd come for her. But, whoever the man was, he'd kept his distance. There'd been no one and nothing to stop her getting on the northbound train.

She looked in the mirror and grimaced at her shadowed eyes and pinched mouth. She'd better get out her make-up.

Tonight was her last night. Tomorrow she'd leave for Australia. She was determined to put on a pretty dress and treat herself to a nice meal and a glass of wine at that cosy restaurant across the square. She'd pretend she was just another tourist enjoying a night out.

Instead of a woman with a broken heart.

Her teeth sank into her bottom lip but Ally refused to cry. She'd be strong because she had no other choice.

A rap on the door made her swing around, frowning. She didn't know anyone here except the staff and they'd have no reason to come to her room at this time.

She unlatched the door, opened it and sucked in a hissed breath. Her pulse thundered in her ears.

'Angelo?'

In the dim light of the hall he was little more than a silhouette, yet totally unmistakable. Proud head, broad shoulders and that utterly masculine frame in a dark suit tailored to his superb body.

Ally's mouth dried and she swallowed convulsively, trying to make sense of him, here, when her brain told her she must be dreaming.

Was she hallucinating? Was this some delayed

reaction to her head injury? Maybe she'd begun seeing things.

'Ally.'

Her skin tightened all over and something swooped low in her belly at the sound of her name on his tongue. It wasn't his rich, melting caramel voice. It was rough-edged and a little husky as if he hadn't spoken much lately. Yet that single word undid her. It made her think of midnight loving and raw desire. Of warmth, passion and the love welling up inside that she couldn't suppress.

Ally's eyes widened and her knees weakened with the force of that emotion. She tightened her grip on the door to keep upright.

He couldn't be here.

'Can I come in?'

He stepped forward and she knew something was wrong. His straight shoulders were unbowed but lines grooved deep around his flattened mouth and the chiselled features that usually looked proud and beautiful seemed too angular.

Instantly Ally stepped back, admitting him.

Yet when she'd closed the door behind him and sagged back against it, Angelo didn't speak, just stood, taking in the small room.

Her skin prickled from the crackling energy he radiated. It was as if her body came alive in his presence and that terrified her. How could she pretend to be immune?

'Angelo?' She found her voice. 'What are you doing here?'

It must be something important for him to come so far. He must have spent a lot of money to track her down.

He swung around, his brooding gaze locking on hers. Ally felt it in the band of heat that tightened around her chest, impairing her breathing. And the leap of her foolish heart.

'I'm not pregnant,' she blurted, not sure where the words came from, or even if they were true, since it was too early to know.

Yet that was the only reason he could be here, to check if there were *consequences* from their one night together.

Was it so important to Angelo to cross off that possibility? To ensure there was nothing left to bind them together? Her mouth turned down on the thought.

'You're not?'

He frowned and Ally told herself her imagination made him sound disappointed.

She hiked her chin up. 'That's why you followed me, isn't it?'

Or could it be something altogether different? Maybe he wanted Alexa's contact details. Maybe he'd finally realised it wasn't hate he felt for her sophisticated cousin but love. That was why he'd been attracted to Ally and why he'd taken her to bed.

She took a deep, shuddery breath and saw his attention drop down her body.

Looking down, she saw her thin robe gaping open from neck to hem, revealing a swathe of pale skin. Fumbling, heat searing her cheeks, Ally covered herself, twisting the belt into a tighter knot.

Angelo's gaze rose, slowly, and she felt it like the brush of his hand, warm, deliberate and arousing, from her belly to her breasts and up her throat. While at the apex of her thighs her pulse thrummed a heavy, needy beat.

She couldn't take this any more. 'I—'

'That's not why I came.' If Angelo's voice had sounded husky before, it was frayed now, a gravelly rasp of sound that abraded every nerve-ending and set her hormones jangling.

'I'll send you Alexa's phone number when I'm in Australia. I don't have it with me.'

Angelo looked blank. 'Alexa's phone number? Why would I want that?'

Ally gathered the lapels of her robe close, wrapping her other arm around her middle. 'I thought…'

His eyebrows rose. 'You thought I want to talk to her?'

He sounded horrified, or was that her imagination playing games?

Ally lifted one shoulder. 'I know you feel strongly about her.'

'Dead right. I never want to see her again.'

'I don't believe you.' She met his stare and refused to be cowed by the frown gathering on his forehead. 'There's something about her you can't get out of your system. Look at the way you were attracted to me. You even had sex with me because you thought I was her.'

'Made love.'

'Sorry?'

'It might have started out as sex, but in the end we made love together.'

Ally's brow scrunched in a frown. 'I don't understand what—'

'Believe me, *tesoro*, there's a difference.' He took a step closer, his dark gaze pinioning hers. 'Sex is a purely physical act but making love…' He lifted his shoulders, spreading his palms wide. 'It's about much more than a physical act and it matters a whole lot more.'

Angelo swallowed and it struck Ally out of nowhere that he looked uncomfortable. More than uncomfortable. On edge. She wanted to read special significance into that but didn't dare let herself. Despite what he seemed to imply.

'You're splitting hairs, Angelo. Just tell me why you're here.'

While she still had the strength to pretend his presence didn't affect her. By her calculations that would be all of three minutes.

His mouth quirked up at one side as if in reluctant amusement. 'Trust you to cut straight to the chase, *amore mio*.' Then his amusement faded and his expression grew serious again. 'I came here because of *you*. I can't let you go. I didn't try to stop you leaving because I knew you needed time and space to deal with everything you've been through. But there are things I have to say, things you need to hear.'

Ally stared up into his strained, handsome face and wondered if she dared trust her ears. This was too like one of those fantasies that she hadn't been able to stop imagining, no matter how hard she tried.

Pride rose to her aid. 'I'm not a substitute for Alexa. And I'm not some obligation or responsibility. I might have washed ashore on your beach but I don't need your protection or your guilt.'

Angelo's head snapped back as if slapped.

'You think I feel...obliged to look out for you?'

'You said it yourself. You have an overdeveloped protective streak. But I'm not a member of your family, Angelo.' Hurt resonated deep inside. 'I'm not some duty to be taken care of.'

Dark eyes held hers and a quiver of longing engulfed her.

'I do want to look after you, Ally, but I fully understand you're strong and independent and you don't *need* me to protect you.' His voice dipped strangely. 'As for being a substitute for Alexa, never! It's true that in the beginning I believed you were her but that's not why I'm attracted to you and definitely *not* why I made love to you.'

Stunned, she gaped at him, watching him rub a hand around the back of his neck as if, like her, his muscles bunched too tight.

'Your resemblance to Alexa kept me at a distance initially. It's the *differences* between you that attract me. Your personality, your mind, your attitude and generosity. That's why I care for you. That's why I want to be with you.'

'You *care* for me?'

Ally's death grip on her collar tightened till her fingers ached.

'I do.' Angelo lifted his arms in a wide shrug. 'I practised what I'd say to you all the way here but I've forgotten all my prepared words.'

She blinked. He was dangerously persuasive as it was.

At the look in his eyes, lush heat spread through her taut body in rolling waves. It was a look Ally had never seen before. Like wonder and desperation and something far more profound, all rolled together.

Her heartbeat quickened as he stepped closer.

'What Alexa and I shared was shallow and brief. It would have ended a lot sooner except business was frantic and I spent a lot of time away from her. I was about to end things when she announced she was pregnant.'

He breathed deep and went on. 'It was *you* I made love to that night, Ally, not some memory of your cousin as you seem to think. For the record, I find you infinitely more desirable than I ever found Alexa. And while you might have been the virgin that night, I can tell you it was a first for me too. It was the first time I *made love* to a woman with my mind, body *and* heart.'

He paused and she heard his harsh breathing, as if from supreme exertion. Or strong feelings.

A perfect match for the raw emotion welling up inside her.

'I've never connected with any other woman like that, ever.'

Dumbfounded, Ally watched his hand cover his heart and her heart melted in response.

'Laugh if you like, but it's true.' His deep voice

grated across sensitive flesh, leaving her trembling with shock and excitement. 'I've held back from emotional relationships because I feared they would make me weak. I saw my mother's pain when my father died, saw the way it almost killed her, and was terrified of the same thing happening to me. *That's* the real reason I've only wanted short affairs before now, not, as I told myself, because I was too busy with work.' He paused, his gaze holding hers. 'Yet with you I tumbled into love in just a week and that's not going to change.'

Ally licked her lips, wondering if she could find her voice. There must be more she needed to ask because surely this was too much to believe. Her heart was hammering and it felt as if a whole flock of swallows swooped and dived in her abdomen.

All that emerged, in a mere scratch of sound, was, 'It's not going to change?'

He shook his head, that rich espresso gaze pinioning her in a way that rooted her to the spot.

'Never. I might be new to love, Ally, but I'm sure. This isn't a passing fancy. This is the real thing. And it's not about duty. It's about what's in my heart.'

He paused and, dazed, she watched his chest rise high on a deep breath. 'The question is whether you feel anything for me. Whether, given time, you might come to care for me too. I know this is sudden and you're still adjusting to having your memory back. I know you've been through a lot and I have no right to push—'

Ally tumbled forward, hands to his chest, face upturned and body flush against his so that all his heat began seeping into her, melting the frost that had turned her bones brittle.

On tiptoe she lifted her face, curled one hand around the back of his neck and pulled his mouth down on hers.

She saw wide, stunned eyes, felt his jolt of surprise. Then there was nothing but the taste of Angelo, luscious on her tongue, the lemony cedar masculine scent of him in her nostrils, his tall frame against her, powerful thighs shifting wider as he drew her in hard and yet harder, until it felt as if they were one. Almost.

Ravenously she kissed him, one hand anchored in the luxuriant hair at the back of his skull, the other slipping beneath his jacket to splay across his shirt and the warm contours of his chest. She swiped his pectoral muscle and felt him shudder as her thumbnail brushed his nipple.

'Ally.'

Even muffled the sound of him saying her name made her heart fly. She smiled against his mouth. Her world had turned on its head in mere moments.

Firm hands planted on her hips, holding her, as Angelo stepped back, breaking their kiss.

'Don't go!' She was beyond caring that she sounded needy. She was beyond anything but the craving for this remarkable, unexpected man.

'I'm not going anywhere.' His glittering eyes had a hungry glaze that made her insides squirm with delight. 'But I don't want to rush you.'

'Rush me?' He had to be kidding. She'd done nothing but yearn for him from the day she'd left. 'I'm crazy for you, Angelo. I've been so lost without you. Not because I wasn't capable of managing on my own, but because I left part of myself with you and never thought I'd get it back.'

That possessive look in his eyes softened into something that made everything inside her go still.

'*Amore mio.*'

There it was again, that delicious *dulce de leche* voice that flowed like hot caramel through her veins and melted her bones.

'Please, Angelo. Show me.'

Those powerful hands didn't hold her back now as she moved in close, nor when she nudged him against the bed.

Instead his mouth curved knowingly as he

wrapped his arms around her and fell back onto the mattress. He rolled and a moment later she was pressed into the bed with him sprawled above her.

There was nowhere else on earth she'd rather be. 'I feel like all my Christmases have come at once.'

Angelo's smile was tender though his body was rigid with arousal. 'I know the feeling. I can't believe I'm so lucky. We've known each other such a short time and it was mired in misunderstanding. I thought I'd have to fight even to have you hear me out.'

'I'm listening.' Her fingers reached for his top button, delight and excitement fizzing like champagne bubbles in her blood. 'But you're wearing too much.'

'There's a remedy for that,' Angelo murmured as he shrugged out of his jacket and ripped his shirt open.

Ally sighed and palmed her hands across his hard chest, enjoying the contrast of silky skin and crisp chest hair.

'Shall I tell you now all the reasons we should stay together?'

His sultry voice was hot temptation whispering in her ear, making her shiver.

'Soon.'

The sight and feel of him distracted her. Her hands dipped to his belt and Angelo's breath caught on a hiss.

Minutes later, after a flurry of movement, they were naked, breathing hard and fast, looking into each other's eyes as their bodies settled against each other.

Her restless hands swept his flanks and up over his broad back. Would she ever get used to the sheer magnificence of this man? 'You feel so good.'

Angelo lowered his head, rubbing his nose against hers, then peppering her eyelids, ears and jaw with tiny kisses. 'That's my line, beautiful Alison.'

She sighed, the breath stalling in her lungs when he swept one hand to the apex of her thighs and into the slippery heat there. Instantly she lifted her hips, pressing into his touch.

'Amore mio. I love how you want me too. I love everything about you.'

His voice was spiky with emotion, making Ally reach up to cup his face in her hands, tenderness filling her. Angelo's eyes shone so brightly, she felt she could fall into those rich depths and stay there for ever.

She shivered as a rising tide of desire, gratitude and love flooded her. The best, most remarkable part was seeing those same emotions in Angelo's face. She felt them in every reverent touch, every careful breath.

Slowly they joined, gazes locked, and Ally felt as if together they entered into one of life's most profound mysteries. As they moved together their tender touches grew more needy, movements quicker and their breathing turned to gasps as rapture exploded, flinging them into bliss.

Yet through it all, the carnal joy and the ecstasy, was a poignant sense of coming home to where she belonged.

A lifetime later they lay, spent and dreamy, in each other's arms.

'I love you, Angelo,' she said when she finally found her voice. Yet she saw his brow knot. 'You don't believe me?'

He raised her hand to his mouth and brushed a kiss to her knuckles. 'I do. But you've just got your memory back. You're in the process of adjusting to your past and who you are. You need time to be sure.'

'I *am* sure, Angelo. You're not the only one who's never felt this way before.'

Still he looked too serious. She reached up and rubbed her finger over the crease that formed above his nose.

'You're not convinced.' She sighed and stretched,

surprised to discover awareness build again as she shifted against his naked body. He felt so amazing. 'Maybe,' she murmured, 'you feel the need to remind me again why being with you is a good idea.'

Ally let her hand slide from his face, down his throat to his chest and lower. Angelo's hand caught hers as she traced an intriguing muscle near his hip.

'Remind you?' he growled and tiny sparks of fire ignited all along her backbone at that sound of pure masculine promise.

'Well, I *have* had memory troubles.' She pouted up at him, trying to stop the grin that threatened to break out. 'You don't want to take any chances on me forgetting, do you?'

'Absolutely not.' His expression turned from tender to voracious in the blink of an eye. A moment later his lips closed around her nipple, making her gasp and arch up against him.

Ally gazed at the man who'd won her heart and soul. 'I think you're onto something there,' she whispered unsteadily.

The wicked gleam in his eyes undid her even more than his erotic caress. 'You're right. I need to know you're sure about us together. I'll have to remind you regularly, over a long time.'

Ally threaded her fingers through his dark hair and grinned at the man she loved. 'That sounds like an excellent plan.'

EPILOGUE

ALLY STOOD ON the wide terrace as the sky began to darken to purple and indigo, feeling the end-of-day warmth seep up through her soles from the sun-warmed flagstones.

She breathed deep, inhaling the rich scent of lavender from the rolling fields beyond the lavish gardens. It mingled with the heady perfume of roses, jasmine and a hundred other flowers blooming in the garden.

It was her favourite time of day, the view over fields and valleys to distant hills lit with the last glowing daylight. Angelo's wedding gift had been this beautiful antique villa on the mainland with an adjacent lavender farm. His thoughtfulness and generosity had almost undone her, for in the process he'd changed his life to accommodate her dreams.

Now, after two years, the house had been renovated to suit them, her business was taking shape and they still managed weekends away at their special island retreat. Angelo telecommuted a lot more and when he went to the city for a few days Ally usually went with him.

She couldn't believe how lucky she was. Not just to be here, but to have Angelo in her life.

She shivered suddenly, thinking of the unlikely circumstance that had brought them together. It would have been so easy for her to visit Italy and never meet him.

'You're cold?' A deep voice sounded behind her and strong arms slid around her, holding her close.

Ally grinned as Angelo's lovely heat enveloped her.

'Not any longer.'

She leaned back in her husband's hold as his hand settled lightly on her purple-blue silk dress, covering the tiny swell of her abdomen.

Ever since she'd shared her news he hadn't been able to stop touching her there, as if still not quite able to take in the fact that they were going to have a child.

She turned in her husband's arms. He looked a million dollars in his tailored dark jacket and his crisp shirt undone at the throat. Ally loved that V of olive-gold skin there, so tempting. But nowhere near as tempting as the soft light in his gleaming eyes.

'What is it, *amore mio*?'

She shrugged. 'I've just been counting my blessings. Thinking how incredibly lucky I was to wash up on your particular beach on that particular day when you were there.'

'Luck?' Ebony eyebrows arched as he shook his head. 'Not luck. It was fate. We were destined for each other. Don't you understand that yet?'

'Oh, really?' She suppressed a delighted smile. 'Yet you refused to marry me for a full year after we met.'

Not that she was annoyed. She'd understood and been touched by Angelo's need to be sure he wasn't rushing her. He'd insisted on giving her time to get her bearings and be absolutely sure that she loved him. He'd even accompanied her back to Australia for a long visit to see family and friends and sort out her affairs.

Angelo's hands moved, roving across the thin silk of her new dress in a way that made her body spark with arousal and her breath hitch. 'Ah, but didn't you enjoy being courted?'

'Is that what you call it? It felt like pure seduction to me.'

His mouth widened into a slow smile she could only describe as wolfish, and a trickle of heat beaded down her spine and dipped low in her abdomen. 'Whatever works, *tesoro*, to keep you happy.'

'*You* make me happy, Angelo. Always you.'

She read the profound emotion in his eyes and

felt her heart swell. 'And I never knew I could be so happy, *amore mio*. Because of *you*.'

He leaned down, his lips about to brush hers when a door slammed and a babble of voices echoed through the house. Someone called their names and Angelo paused, whispering words under his breath that Ally, with her improving Italian, knew weren't for public consumption.

'Whose idea was it to have a party tonight?' he growled.

Ally laughed. 'Yours, darling. You said I should invite all our friends and your family to celebrate my birthday. And unless I'm mistaken Giulia and your mother have arrived with some of your cousins. Or maybe that's Oliver's deep voice I hear in the distance.'

'Branston?' Angelo's pulled her in closer. 'The man always flirts with you outrageously. I think he sometimes forgets you're a married woman. I have to watch him like a hawk.'

But Ally read the glint of humour in her husband's eyes. 'And I think you just like an excuse to keep me close.'

He grinned disarmingly and her heart gave a little flutter of pure delight. 'You know me so well, *tesoro*.'

Angelo ignored the approaching voices and swept her back over his arm, settling his mouth over hers in a passionate yet tender kiss that made her silently agree that their meeting really had been destined. Because there was no other explanation for such perfect joy.

* * * * *

LET'S TALK

Romance

For exclusive extracts, competitions and special offers, find us online:

📘 facebook.com/millsandboon

📷 @millsandboonuk

🐦 @millsandboon

Or get in touch on 0844 844 1351*

For all the latest titles coming soon, visit millsandboon.co.uk/nextmonth

Want even more
ROMANCE?

Join our bookclub today!

'Mills & Boon books, the perfect way to escape for an hour or so.'

Miss W. Dyer

'Excellent service, promptly delivered and very good subscription choices.'

Miss A. Pearson

'You get fantastic special offers and the chance to get books before they hit the shops'

Mrs V. Hall

Visit millsandbook.co.uk/Bookclub and save on brand new books.

MILLS & BOON